STRONGER THAN *Fate*

BECCA SEYMOUR

RAINBOW TREE PUBLISHING

PRAISE FOR BECCA SEYMOUR

Good guys, bad guys, twists, it's all there. Add in the excellent writing and general story-telling, and all you have to do is wrap it up in a bow.

JERRI, AMAZON REVIEW

So many heart-pounding surprises and intense reveals!

DEVOTED♡READER

Such a great urban fantasy series!

AMAZON REVIEW

For snarky relationships and those people who know how to support you without even needing to ask.

STRONGER THAN FATE

FANGS & FELONS
BOOK 4

BECCA SEYMOUR

RAINBOW TREE PUBLISHING

ALSO BY BECCA SEYMOUR

Zone Defense

No Take Backs | No More Secrets | No Wrong Moves | No Backing Down

Fast Break

Rules, Schmules! | Facts, Smacts! | Regular Smegular! | Easy, Schmeasy!

True-Blue

Let Me Show You | I've Got You | Becoming Us | Thinking It Over | Always For You | It's Not You | Our First & Last | Next For Us

Outback Boys

Stumble | Bounce | Wobble

Fangs & Felons

Thicker Than Water | Weaker Than Instinct | Brighter Than Fear | Stronger Than Fate

Stand-Alone Contemporary

Not Used To Cute | High Alert | Realigned | Amalgamated | Under the Blazing Stars | Best Kind of Awkward | Tastes Like Sugar

EDITING: HOT TREE EDITING

COVER DESIGNER: BOOKSMITH DESIGN

PUBLISHER: RAINBOW TREE PUBLISHING

E-BOOK ISBN: 978-1-922679-80-2

PAPERBACK ISBN: 978-1-923252-11-0

CHAPTER 1
LUCAS

THE EXPLOSION VIBRATED AROUND THE ROOM WITH A deafening roar. The walls shook. A painting rattled. My usually slow-beating heart raced as I clenched my fists, the noise growing louder with each passing second.

The tightening of my fists was the only thing keeping me in check. That and the counting in my head.

I'd lost track of how many times I'd tried to count to ten.

Another boom and my patience snapped.

"Seriously, Wilder. Switch it off or put on those damn headphones."

The explosion echoed again. This time the bottle on the table rattled.

One. Two. Three—

A loud scream pierced the air. That of a soldier losing a limb.

That was exactly what was going to happen to Ethan bloody Wilder if he didn't heed my warning and switch off the damn game. My patience was paper-thin. Hell, it had a BMI less than that.

What the hell was thinner than tissue paper beyond my patience and nerves?

"Wilder." It was rare that I growled. Even rarer that my fangs extended. The itch in my gums warned me they were close to the surface, eager to tear out the bear's throat.

I'd drain him dry, and beyond the slurps and the sound of me stamping on the gaming device, nothing but the beautiful sound of a slowing heartbeat would be my soundtrack.

Maybe then I'd be able to get on with figuring out where Hornell was—the former captain who remained the annoying thorn in my side at the top of the Supernatural Investigation Crime Bureau's Most Wanted list.

That and I'd make the bullshit warrants out on me and my team in the Infiltration Tactical Unit disappear. Though not without taking the heads of the corrupt individuals who'd allowed it to happen.

For a vampire, I wasn't usually so bloodthirsty— ironic for sure—but I still hadn't decided if I would do that metaphorically or if I would put them in the ground.

If Callen, my division leader, had his way, it would be the latter.

The sound of blood splattering against the screen with a dramatic grunt of an alien being wounded by a spray of bullets finally did it.

In four strides, I reached the plug socket and yanked the lead.

Exquisite silence.

Which lasted for barely a second before Wilder pounced out of the chair, the movement fast and completely at odds with his huge bulk.

"The fuck you do that for, tosser?"

Angling my head up to stare him dead in the eyes, I huffed out a frustrated breath. "I can't think with all the stupid blasting. You have a headset. Use it."

"I would, but I need to listen out for intruders as well."

"All you had to do was turn the volume down, and we wouldn't have a problem. You're being an inconsiderate arsehole." Any semblance of calm disappeared. My voice shook, my anger vibrating under my skin.

"It was the only way to block out your pacing and heavy breathing," Wilder spat.

"Heavy breathing?!" I shouted incredulously. *What the ever-loving fuck?* "I breathe once a minute, if that, you ignoramus. And I'm hardly pacing."

Admittedly, I may have been pacing a little, but it was day three of us being trapped together in one of my safe houses outside Brisbane.

We were holed up in the residence I had on Tamborine Mountain. It provided good coverage surrounded by rainforest and had plenty of boltholes and numerous exits should the need arise.

But rather than Wilder being grateful for the safe house or the well-stocked fridge I'd organised or even the comfortable king-size bed that easily supported his giant frame, he grumbled and complained like being here was a hardship.

I clenched my jaw, staring daggers at him.

A hardship would have been me abandoning him at the private airstrip just south of Brisbane and leaving him to fend for himself in a foreign-to-him country with a warrant out for him to be taken into custody for questioning by the bureau.

"Puh-*lease*." The word was all derision. "You're practically wearing a hole in the floorboards while you're huffing *and* puffing. You're even mumbling to yourself." Wilder's shoulders eased a fraction, and the barest of smiles appeared on his lips. He angled forwards, a full-on smirk on his face that was all menace and enjoyment as he aimed to get a rise out of me.

I knew what the arsehole was attempting.

"How old did you say you were again? Maybe you're finally losing the plot. I've heard stories about old vampires losing their marbles. I'll get you a chain you can rattle if you want to keep pacing."

"That's ghosts." My lip curled into a sneer.

It was hard not to bite. Not to push back like I knew he wanted.

The flip in him—the switch from reactive anger to him goading me, looking for a fight—wasn't the first over the past three days. Hell, it'd happened even before that, when we'd been at Hart's place.

The urge to give Wilder what he wanted, to react to the aggression he craved, burned deep in my gut. Not a chance I'd give him that satisfaction. Not only because he was pissing me off, but also because this house had cost a small fortune to kit out to my specs.

The thought was the reminder I needed.

I refused to buckle. I wasn't here to babysit or play games with Wilder and his grizzly's instincts.

What we needed was to clear our names, shut down the bullshit case against my team, and put Hornell behind bars or in the ground. It was rare I opted for the latter, but the growing body count Hornell was responsible for and, quite frankly, the abhorrent experimentation and projects he fronted meant his death would be justly deserved.

"Ghosts, huh? Really?"

Bloody hell. Why did I even respond to "correct" him? Talk about allowing myself to be dragged in.

I worked hard at relaxing my tight muscles, when what I wanted to do was close my eyes, throw my head back, and cuss him out. Perhaps beg for divine intervention. But I wouldn't give him the satisfaction of letting him know how much he rattled me.

With the exception of tearing the plug from the wall socket.

I had my limits.

Focussing on getting my composure back, I stepped towards the workstation, saying, "Did you get the information you were looking for?" I sort of kept the bite from my question.

Working in the back office, I'd been neck deep in calls on a secure line to Callen, the SICB division leader and my friend. We'd been discussing more sensitive details about past ITU cases that Wilder most definitely didn't have the clearance for.

Not that he had any clearance.

Hell, neither did I, for that matter, since I was underground, staying clear of the SICB agents instructed to bring me and my unit in.

Thankfully, Callen's name wasn't attached to any

of the leaked files—nor the bullshit ones. While he used to be a part of the team, his appointment to division leader happened over two years ago. The files making their rounds didn't appear to go back that far. It was a stroke of luck that he maintained his position and was able to act as our eyes and ears while the rest of the team were scattered around Australia, hiding out.

"I'm just waiting for a contact to get back to me. I took a break to clear my head."

I bit my tongue from making a snide remark about the noise and sat down, my back to him.

"It looks like your team's files made it to the ShadowNet before Hart was able to take it down."

I froze, stomach bottoming out. Turning slowly, I faced him. "What?"

"I said—"

I frowned and shook my head, cutting him off. Making zero attempts at keeping the bite out of my tone, I snapped, "I know what you said. I'm just wondering why you're only telling me this now."

This man was going to be the death of me.

That he would sit on crucial information that put my team at risk while he indulged in mindless gaming was beyond frustrating.

Once again, my gums itched. As did my trigger finger.

Staring at me, seeming completely unaffected, Wilder didn't even offer a shrug.

"Just to be clear. You discovered this information yet decided to play a stupid fucking game instead?" I seethed, my hands clenching at my sides. "There are some serious fucking consequences, not only to my team but also their families. Lives could be ruined or taken because you prioritised playing over having a simple conversation with me."

Not even a flicker of remorse registered in his gaze. "Gaming helps me think. My brain needed a rest while I figured out the best course of action." His unrepentant voice, almost at the point of monotone, simply fuelled my frustration.

Dead. He was going to be the deadest bear that ever died.

"Think?" The vein in my temple throbbed. "Think?" My voice rose. Putting my claws around his thick neck would be beyond satisfying. "While our entire operation hangs by a thread, you were *thinking* by blowing shit up?"

"Killing aliens, actually." This time, a one-shouldered shrug punctuated his words.

Turning my back to him, I paced, trying to contain the rage bubbling inside me. "You know what? I'll handle damage control. You just go back to your precious game."

"You're so dramatic. Geez." An over-the-top sigh escaped him.

Me? Dramatic?

Okay, so I was admittedly close to tearing his head off, but while he may have no allegiances or responsibility, I did.

Heck, that pretty much summed up my life. My whole existence.

The vein in my temple pulsed, my headspace struggling to find room for all that needed to be done.

"That's the information I'm waiting for from my contact. They're providing some coding that will allow me to not only pull the data but also track who's accessed it," Ethan said.

I stopped short, my focus returning to him as he continued to speak.

"You know how impossible that should be, right?"

Shit, I really did.

All my fight evaporated. "You have a contact who can do that?"

"Yes." A smug smile made its way to his lips.

The expression caught my attention. Did I want to smack the smile from his face? Hell yes. But it wasn't lost on me that, self-satisfied or not, it was the first time I'd seen a smile reach his eyes.

The move somehow brightened his dark brown eyes, shaking away the deep, pissed-off intensity that was usually present. The flash of his white teeth contrasted sharply against the unruly beard that framed his jawline, making him appear frustratingly handsome.

I gritted my teeth, unwilling to acknowledge the pull his smile had on me.

Wilder was trouble. I didn't have time for distractions, especially ones wrapped in a package as aggravatingly bulky and grumpy as him. It shouldn't be charming—him being a cranky arsehole.

Suppressing the urge to roll my eyes, I forced myself to focus on the serious issues at hand. "Well, get them on the line," I demanded, trying to ignore the warmth spreading through me despite my irritation with him.

He quirked his brow before making a show of looking at his watch with sloth-like speed. "They'll be in touch in four minutes. While 'playing games,'" he said pointedly, "I thought of something I want to try that should help us fly under the radar when the tracking software is running. Without it, it won't take long before alarms are ringing and those individuals who've accessed your team's profiles are shutting down and deleting their fingerprints."

I held back my wince. Humble pie tasted like shit,

but sometimes it was necessary to throw some whipped cream on it and eat it all up.

"Thank you. Do you need help?"

Wilder's skill set was phenomenal—he had some serious creative brainpower working for him. Not that I was too shabby with computer software. But working inside the law meant my creative instincts were regularly restricted.

A hacker like Wilder, who, despite his years working for the British Cyber Unit, absolutely no longer worked inside the restraints of the law, was a wholly different breed. As a hacker for hire, he operated in the shadows, bending and breaking the rules with a finesse that left even seasoned cybercrime investigators scratching their heads.

Because of course I'd done my research on him since being holed up for the past three days.

A few days ago, Hart—our "unicorn hacker" who'd fallen for one of my agents, Smythe—had brought him in to assist in a nightmare case that spread deeper, darker, and wider with every minute that passed.

Before then, I'd never known about Ethan Wilder's existence. Why would I when he lived on the other side of the world?

Now, I knew a lot more. Though I suspected

Wilder could redact information he didn't want me or anyone else to know.

I couldn't help but be grudgingly impressed.

Despite my reservations about his methods, his approach was effective. He got things done, no matter how illegal and morally questionable they might be.

Yet, that was also why he was caught up in this drama in the first place: his involvement in assisting Hornell.

Because of that, I couldn't fully trust him. He'd pleaded his case and promised his "innocence" as far as how deep his involvement went. But still, I wouldn't let down my guard.

What was probably even worse was that the situation we were in meant I was officially on the run. Every day I didn't turn myself in for questioning, I broke the law.

Talk about ironic.

Wilder's "No" to my offer of help was part scoff, part confusion.

Whatever.

I sat back down in front of my computer system, viscerally aware of Wilder sitting a metre away on my right.

While waiting, I'd check on Shaw and Michaels.

They'd been in Brisbane when the alert for us to be taken in for questioning had been triggered.

I absolutely regretted parting ways, wishing they'd come here with us to act as a buffer rather than heading to another of my safe houses south of Gympie, about three hours north. A small light-aircraft airport close by meant they had options if they needed to make a quick exit.

After logging into the encrypted server, I shot them a request for a welfare status report.

Their reply was immediate: *Safe*.

They were working on their contacts, trying to find a location on Hornell. Once they had something —a possible lead—I'd be the first to know.

The sound of Wilder's fingers flying over the keyboard drew my attention.

I glanced at his screen. "That them?"

"Nah, it's my neighbour asking for me to pick her up a battered sausage from the chippie."

Sarcastic arsehole.

"Yeah." He sighed, no doubt hearing me grit my teeth. He hit a few more keys. "They've managed to get the coding sorted. I'm going to add my own special blend of magic to it. Then we'll get this bad boy running."

The glee in his voice was at complete odds with every other tone he'd used.

And I got it.

Chubbing up over tech or coding that was hands down a beautiful masterpiece had happened to me a time or two over the years. His voice, though, while already gruff, had an extra layer of gravel. Hell, an air of whimsy coated his words.

He must be pretty impressed with himself.

Not that I wasn't.

"Fucking magic," he said with glee, punching in some numbers before stretching his large arms above his head and easing back in the leather chair. The metal structure creaked at the movement.

He was a seriously built guy—all barrel-chested and long limbs. At six foot six, he towered over me.

Pulling my attention away from his bare fore-arms, which were smattered with dark hair, I zeroed in on his computer monitor.

Excitement clenched my heart, holding it firmly in its grasp as the program appeared to be doing exactly what it was created to do.

While I was pissed that the data had made its way to the ShadowNet, pulling my focus—albeit briefly—away from finding Hornell and trying to discover the hold he had over the government officials Murdock and Jefferson, I was grateful Wilder discovered the breach.

Even more so that he'd come up with a solution and was dealing with it.

Being the boss could be isolating. While I treated my team with respect and care, work mode was my default setting. Part of that was always thinking, planning, and trying to stay two steps ahead.

That was no slight to my team. They were competent and followed leads without prompting, but I was involved in their decisions.

Wilder taking the lead was as disconcerting as it was liberating.

The thought pulled me up short.

Liberating?

What the ever-loving hell?

Oblivious to the direction of my alarming thoughts, Wilder continued to veg out in the leather chair like he was kicking back in front of the TV.

What must it be like to be so laid-back and chilled, behaving like you didn't have a care in the world?

He shot bolt upright. While I could only see the side of his profile, I saw enough to recognise the incredulity.

"What is it? What's wrong?" I moved my chair close, almost within touching distance, and received a whiff of his scent: spring forests after a light shower.

Somehow keeping my expression neutral at my observation, I focussed intently on his screen.

Four windows highlighted different data—two static and the other two moving with fresh information.

"What's that?" I pressed, trying to absorb as much of the information as possible. Data, in general, I could handle, just like I could coding, but even with my specialism in the creation of tech, which honestly was more like a hobby and had earned me a pretty penny over the years, I struggled to know what I was looking at.

Not that I'd tell Wilder that.

"Someone's online right now, trying to access the files."

"Can you stop them?"

A fast look at me and I pressed my lips together. A bubble of ill-timed amusement tried to break free at Wilder's expression that morphed into a blend of disbelief and irritation. His jaw tightened, eyes narrowing at me.

His gaze bored into me with a mix of annoyance and superiority, as if the very notion of questioning his abilities was preposterous.

Choosing to keep my mouth shut and liking a little too much that I was able to get a rise from him, I simply gave a chin lift towards the screen.

His "of course I can stop them, why do you even doubt me" look stayed in place a second longer before he turned his focus to his keyboard. Another smug smile settled on his lips, capturing my attention. *Fascinating.* It seriously was.

This grumpy bear had a hair-trigger mood switch. Why I found that as fun as it was riveting was all levels of worrying. No doubt because I'd lost count of the years since another person had stirred any reaction in me.

"Done."

I barely held back my body jerk, having been lost in his focussed, gleeful expression while he'd been working.

"I've even tracked their location. I've put it on the central encrypted server you pointed me to earlier."

Impressed, I bobbed my head. "Thank you."

"I didn't do it for you."

The creak of my molars grinding filled my ears. Maybe if I concentrated on that, I wouldn't decapitate him. *That* was how far he pushed me.

I knew better than to bite, than to react to his snide remarks and sarcasm-laced digs, but….

"So why did you do it?"

The question had played through my mind so many times over the past three days. Even before that when we were at Hart's warehouse.

Wilder turned in the swivel chair to face me, then studied me with an intensity that would likely have made a lesser agent shrivel.

Not me.

I'd spent longer than a lifetime under the scrutiny of dominant supernaturals. I'd worked hard at erasing several in particular from my memory while fighting to never feel cowed or overpowered again.

A grumpy bear would need to try a lot harder to successfully intimidate me. And his size.... I shook any thoughts of his vastness away. Large, muscular, thick, and tall were all elements of my personal kryptonite that I couldn't think too deeply about.

Probably because he was the polar opposite of the nightmare I'd lived with in the past.

Instead, embracing his anger, his indifference, or whatever mood he fired my way remained the safest option.

For Wilder too.

He just didn't know it.

Just when I considered rolling back to my station, he parted his lips, saying, "That kid Hart's all over— he didn't deserve what happened to him."

Surprise kept me quiet.

"I'm not going to justify why I take on the jobs I do, but I am all levels of pissed off that I wasn't fully aware of the specifics of the chip or the program that

I designed for Hornell. The name wasn't anywhere within a thousand miles of this. And I always do my due fucking diligence."

For the first time since speaking, he cast a steady glance my way. "If none of you want to believe me," he said with a shrug, "then that's on you. I don't give two shits."

We held eye contact for a long beat. Confusion swirled in every available space in my body.

Did I believe him? Not that he cared either way, apparently. But still, did I?

His shock when he'd first arrived at Hart's warehouse had appeared real. And would I have brought him with me, to one of my safe houses, if I thought he was a genuine risk? Likely not.

Something niggled, though. Didn't quite sit right. Though I didn't expect I'd be getting any answers, which made sense because unravelling Ethan Wilder and discovering what kind of man he was, let alone his secrets, was not in my top ten list of priorities. Not right now.

A beep from his monitor dragged our attention to it.

Wilder tensed immediately, his fingers flying across the keys as I inched in closer to his side. Alarm pulsed through my veins as I committed each detail to memory, absorbing the words his coding had been set in to alert us should we be at risk.

At risk?

There was an almost maniacal bubble of laughter wedged in my throat, threatening to burst free.

I never lost my shit in public. Never lost control with someone else present.

At risk didn't even begin to cover it.

I leapt out of my seat and raced to my station to punch in the coding for lockdown.

My systems would be fried, with the exception of the two laptops in my go bag and the collection of equipment already in the back of my SUV.

"We've got to move." I half expected my inappropriate snicker to burst free. Relieved I'd contained it, I snatched my keys and stood in front of my security system. "How long?"

"Seven minutes." Wilder was out of his chair, one hand on his keyboard, the other typing on his phone.

While questions buzzed around my head concerning how on earth we'd been discovered, it wasn't the time. Instead, I focussed on my security system. The SICB would eventually be able to breach my safe house, but I wouldn't make it easy on them.

Once I sorted the appropriate lockdowns, I cast a quick glance at Wilder. At his full height, he was impressive. Standing there with his fluffy Cookie

Monster laptop bag under his arm, he was definitely a vision of something.

My lips twitched despite the countdown and the precarious situation.

"What?" Eyes narrowed, he zeroed in on me, just daring me to say something. When I didn't speak, he huffed out a breath. "I got conned into buying raffle tickets for a charity event. I could have bought a thousand of the damn things with how much I paid."

The tightness in my chest loosened a fraction. This was so not the time for any of this.

Five minutes.

I needed to destroy my phone and activate another. I also needed to—

"I've reached out to your team. Told them to be on high alert."

It took me half a beat to nod in acknowledgement. Apparently, Wilder also had mind-reading skills.

I swiped my phone off the table, crushed it in the palm of my hand, and discarded the debris.

"We'll need to get another car. I'm not sure if mine has been compromised," I said, picking up the go bag I kept in my workspace and glancing around the room. The house needed to be locked down so nothing could be salvaged by the SICB, who'd be here any moment.

The fact that they'd found us so quickly was a concern and kept my ego in check.

Four minutes. It was now or never.

"We've got to move."

A firm nod from Wilder, and then he took hold of his laptop, swiped his small travel bag, and was at my side in two large strides.

He took the lead so I could engage the additional security on the room and then the house. Unfortunately, both would eventually be breached. While the security system was my own tech and the best in the exclusive market—no way had I allowed mass production from my patent—the SICB had the details on file.

Because of course I'd shared that intel. Well, 85 percent of it. As my government, the agency I'd dedicated the past few decades to, I'd trusted them almost implicitly.

The *almost* was the reason I'd held back that 15 percent.

Following my gut, which was right in this instance, was a bitter pill to swallow.

Once outside and surrounded by the eucalypt forest, I inhaled the familiar scent—a blend of clean, crisp notes of menthol and pine with a hint of rich earth. But hell if, with the tension vibrating through my body as I looked at the driveway entrance, it didn't carry ominous undertones that had no place here. The fragrance of eucalyptus leaves, though usually soothing, seemed tinged with impending danger.

I paused from heading towards my SUV, not sensing Wilder's large presence.

The hell?

I spun, searching, listening keenly.

A rustle to the side of the house that led into the forest reached me. My muscles tightened, ready for action. I zeroed in on the unfamiliar weight of my sidearm, not used to wearing it. Tingles shot through my fingers as I prepared to move, not wanting to budge an inch as I waited.

Either Wilder had finally wondered what on earth he was doing by still sticking around and had abandoned the mission or…. Hell if I knew what the alternative was.

I needed to move. Get in the SUV and drive away.

The sound, however, kept me rooted. That and my gut told me I needed to be here.

Almost two decades, and it had rarely let me down. Before that was another story, but I hoped my instinct wasn't messing with me.

Branches snapped. Foliage was flattened by a force I couldn't see even as I angled my head to look.

My fingers twitched, still not ready to move to my gun but prepared to do so in an instant.

A heavy huff and a cuss carried in the wind. Immediately, I relaxed.

Wilder.

He emerged from the forest looking like he'd wrestled a croc. Twigs and leaves plastered his hair like a crown more fitting to a nymph than a grizzly bear in biped form. Wilder was always striking, but like this, he was mesmerising, especially when his gaze locked on mine.

"Get your bag out of the SUV," he demanded, his gruffness sparking me into action.

I didn't hesitate about which bags to take. I tugged out the bag full of tech and shoved the backpack I'd brought from the house with me on properly over my shoulders, leaving a second emergency escape kit behind. I raced towards him, eyeing the motorbike he'd pushed out of the forest.

I knew better than to ask the million questions concerning the hows, the whens, the whats, and the whys that were racing through my brain.

To be honest, I shouldn't have been surprised that he was so prepared or that he had the contacts in Australia to organise this.

I eyed the saddlebags, the shoved the tech bag inside one of them and accepted the helmet Wilder passed me with a smug smirk. He removed a second from the handlebars and shoved it unceremoniously onto his head before straddling the bike and starting the engine with the electric switch.

I didn't hesitate.

In approximately one minute, this place would be swarmed. I wanted us to be at a distance and not even able to see them in the side mirrors.

Settling behind him, I barely had the chance to grab hold of his waist before he revved the engine, and we flew down the drive. "Fuck me." The words punched out of me unbidden, and I held tighter.

He barely slowed as he turned onto the road before racing onto a smaller side street. I grunted and absolutely didn't squeal as he made an abrupt left turn onto a track used for dirt bikes.

This wasn't a dirt bike, but hell if Wilder didn't handle it with the ease of one as he weaved around potholes and ruts in the hard dirt.

The bike, a sleek, high-performance sports model better suited for city streets than rugged terrain, seemed to defy its purpose under Wilder's command. Its engine roared with power as he expertly navigated the rough track, effortlessly dodging obstacles that would have thrown a less-skilled rider off course.

The last time I'd been on a bike was likely fifty

years ago. They were not as fast as this back then. An abrupt laugh leapt out of my chest, not only at my ridiculous "back in the day" thought, but fuck, this was fun. While Wilder was a grumpy arsehole and I wanted to strangle him pretty much all the damn time, his riding skills were impressive.

The wind whipped around us as we leaned into sharp turns, the scent of dust and eucalyptus mingling in the air. I held on tight, torn between exhilaration and apprehension, as Wilder guided the bike with precision and confidence that didn't surprise me. There was no denying his reckless nature, but in this moment, his ability to tame the untameable machine beneath us demanded my begrudging respect.

I grinned, relieved he couldn't see or hear me. Sure, our supernatural hearing went a long way, but muffled by helmets and the sound of the engine, plus add in the tyres on dirt and the wind whipping around us, and I basked in the moment of freedom.

A "whoop" was eager to escape, but I swallowed it down, not wanting to risk the volume.

The worry for my team and what this infiltration meant for our mission hovered at the edges of my brain. Neither was something I could do anything about. Not until we were safe. So I leaned into the momentary escape the ride and Wilder provided.

It was clear he knew where he was heading.

One thing for certain, Wilder was a quick study. His escape plan was impeccable. This route would take us out to the west of the mountain. From there, there was little other than farmland and the vast range heading towards Beaudesert, which was just thirty minutes away. Beyond that and farther west was the outback.

There were also numerous small airbases.

I didn't doubt Wilder was privy to all of this. What I was curious about was where his escape plan would take us.

"Where are you heading?" I mumbled, barely paying attention to the passing trees. Before long we'd be on the bitumen. I suspected I'd have a better clue then.

"I've got something set up in Warwick."

I froze at his voice, loud and clear in my helmet.

"We'll be there in under two hours. So feel free to squeal away when I take the bends on one knee."

Heat engulfed me, embarrassment flushing my skin and itching my fingers.

The only cure would be to wrap them around his neck.

The helmets were fitted with a mic and speaker, but not a chance I'd call him out on it. Pleading ignorance was the only play here.

That and saying, "Whatever, arsehole. Just don't crash and give us road rash."

His huff of laughter filled my ears, not at all gravelly or having anything to do with the way my skin pebbled.

I loosened my grip, aware I was holding on to him as tightly as a spider monkey. As soon as I removed one hand and searched for a grip rail behind me, the engine revved higher, the front wheel kicked up, and I had no choice but to launch at Wilder, wrap both arms around him, and hang on.

My "You fucking arsehole" didn't penetrate his gruff laughter. Not one bit.

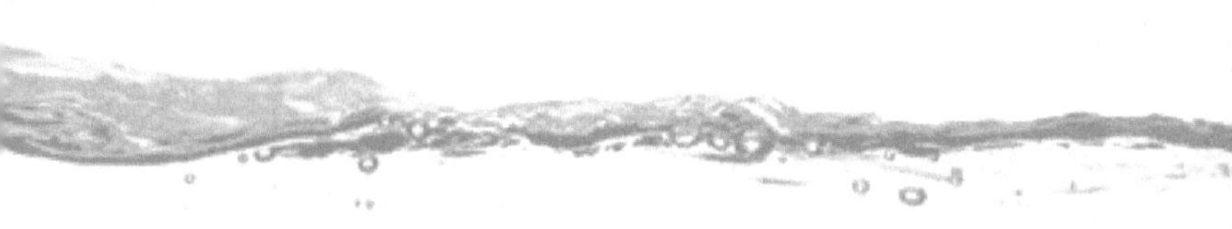

CHAPTER 2
WILDER

THE FURTHER OUT WE RODE, THE DRIER IT BECAME. THE landscape, so different than the English countryside, took some getting used to, but it didn't mean it wasn't striking.

At the vampire's heavy huff right behind me, my lips twitched. We'd been riding west for maybe an hour and forty, but some of those minutes were taken up by the frantic journey off the steep mountainside. Since then, there were no vehicles behind us and no drones in the sky. Considering the vast blue skies, we would have seen any hovering.

With each moment that passed by, I relaxed even as amusement bubbled in my gut. Riling Mathew Lucas up was more entertaining than I ever imagined. Even better, it was ridiculously easy.

What made his agitation so much sweeter, addictive almost, was that I wasn't sure who was more surprised by his inability to keep his reactions to me in check.

Lucas screamed "in control." It had been that way at Hart's warehouse. The vampire had been the epitome of togetherness and efficiency. Considering his team, I understood the need. I suspected it took a lot to rein them in.

And the vampire had worn "bossman" like a second skin.

Until me.

Or rather, until we were alone, thrust into this ridiculous situation because of a corrupt agency—though grudgingly I could admit it was likely individuals rather than a whole agency—and government officials who were greedy fucks.

Because that was likely the reason they'd fallen into bed with the likes of Hornell.

The former captain didn't have any real political or religious affiliations, regardless of his previous allegiance to king and country. Not that I did, either, and I was fuelled by hard cash… or gold if I had my pick.

The difference, though, was that I never intended to hurt people… unless they deserved it. Hornell and every single individual involved with the chaos and destruction both past and present were absolutely on my shit list, their halos so damaged that nothing but red-hot pain and torment lay before them.

I wondered if they knew that already.

The T-junction ahead meant we were getting closer. Bypassing Warwick and steering clear of government cameras was the plan. I'd memorised this journey as soon as I'd been locked in Lucas's safe house. It had been the first thing I'd done—organised plans A, B, and C.

There was no such thing as too many ways out.

When we turned, I felt Lucas's keen observation as he took in our surroundings. A few miles—kilometres… whatever—and we took a sharp turn onto a dirt track, something I'd noticed were plentiful in the Aussie hinterland and countryside.

I grinned when Lucas had no choice but to grip me firmly if he wanted to stay seated.

"A heads-up next time," he grumbled, his voice tight through the helmet's speaker.

I huffed out a snort, confident it would rile him further.

It took ten minutes and two different roads before we reached a gate.

"What is this place?" he asked, stepping off the bike once we'd stopped. He tugged off his helmet, not bothering to straighten his unruly hair. The dark strands stuck up in multiple directions. Dishevelled looked good on him. I sneered at the thought of paying him any sort of compliment, even in my mind. Grudgingly, I acknowledged he was handsome with his sharp jawline and Romanesque nose. There was definitely European blood in his heritage.

There were no bulging muscles in sight—the norm for born vampires. Though I may have stumbled across him wrapped only in a towel yesterday, so I knew his lithe frame and tall limbs were wrapped in sinewy muscle.

At his pointed stare and raised brows, I swallowed down my thoughts of Lucas's tempting body. Nothing good could come of fantasising about things I shouldn't want and couldn't ever have.

"An access code will get us onto the property," I said, getting my mind back on track. "There's a few hundred acres here and only one small house. Closer to the house, there's additional security, including air space alerts to detect drones. It also gives out an electronic pulse to prevent satellite observations."

Immediately, Lucas's brows shot high before he peered over at the innocuous-looking fence. The gate and fence line were standard in these parts. Just barbed wire—though electrified with regulatory warnings.

What there weren't signs about were the sensors or cameras located around the boundary.

It paid to be neck deep in the not-so-legal network I was involved in. This location was one of hundreds around the world that were co-opted. Something for obvious reasons I wouldn't be sharing with Lucas.

While he might have been on the run with a notice out to bring him in for questioning, he was still a law enforcement agent. When all of this bullshit was put to bed, I had no doubt he'd be back to leading his ITU team.

"And this place is what and belongs to who, exactly?"

I paused at the gate I'd reached after dismounting my bike. Shit, it was hella warm here. It was likely I'd sweat my balls clear off my body before I had the chance to fly home.

Not for the first time I wondered what the fuck I was doing here.

I stared at Lucas, having no intention of giving him the answer he sought.

"I see," he responded.

I snorted, the sound loud in the still, empty space. Credit where credit was due: the vamp was a quick study.

I turned my back to him, punched in the code, and followed up with the retinal scan. As I did so, I smirked, imagining what Lucas thought about my ability to access such a location in remote Australia, a country I'd only visited once before.

I was already tugging out my phone when it beeped, so I opened the secure app and typed in the secondary access code. The green approval symbol appeared immediately on my app. Straight after it did, the gates opened, the heavy frames sliding easily despite their lack of use or how basic they appeared.

Nothing about this compound was basic.

Oh shit. The thought smacks me in the face.

While technically nothing about this compound was basic, the shabby-looking house really was small. Sure, inside was a hatch to an underground bunker complete with enough tech to make anyone in my line of work—or Lucas's—get a stiffy. But back to the house. One bedroom. One fucking bed. A functional kitchen-diner, sitting area, and bathroom.

"What's wrong?"

I barely held back my flinch, having zoned out and fixated on the whole one-bed realisation.

In my escape plan, I hadn't exactly factored in Lucas joining me. Truth was, I half expected to need to disappear from him and his team.

Fuck it all to hell.

"Nothing," I grumbled, not wanting to get into anything here. There was nothing either of us could do. It made sense to let him discover the sleeping situation for himself. "Ready?" I didn't check as I returned to the bike, straddled it, and started the engine.

A glance his way and I gritted my teeth. The arsehole simply stood there staring at me.

"Feel free to walk if you want." No skin off my nose if he chose to be a stubborn prick.

His jaw clenched—a tell I didn't expect he revealed very often.

As I turned the throttle, I couldn't shake the smirk that tugged at the corners of my lips, a rush of adrenaline coursing through me like wildfire. It was like playing a game of cat and mouse, and right now, I had the upper hand. It was one hell of an electrifying sensation, a surge of elation that pulsed through my veins, stirring the beast inside me.

My heart pounded against my ribcage, matching the rhythm of the motorbike's roar.

His gaze narrowed, his silent dare right there. A challenge.

Invigorated by the tension crackling in the dense heat between us, I felt alive and far too satisfied. Pushing Lucas's buttons was intoxicating. Was it because he was formidable? Perhaps. It was also because the energy spiking off him when pissed off was sexy as fuck.

The stirring in the pit of my stomach was dangerous, as was the warmth spreading through me like honey. Just the possibility of tasting his sweet nectar was—

Double fuck.

As I glanced at Lucas, I turned the throttle once more and kicked the stand. The tension between us tightened, turned palpable—a silent battle of wills.

He'd be in for a rude awakening if he didn't make a move in the next ten seconds.

His jaw clenched again, a subtle glimpse at the frustration simmering beneath his cool exterior. There was a flicker of something else in his gaze, an awareness that would only spell disaster if it mirrored the heat coursing through my veins.

Nine. Ten.

I revved, knocked the bike into gear, and focussed on the dirt road ahead as I took off. There'd be enough time to unravel—that or completely bury— the tangled mess of emotions swirling inside me. For now, he could walk, turn into a damn bat and fly, or spin around and fuck off in the other direction for all I cared.

I didn't bother looking in my side mirror even as the gates closed behind me.

Lucas would either show up or not. Either way, I wouldn't back down on my promise to Hart—I'd help take Hornell down. I didn't shirk my responsibilities and wouldn't ignore the hand I'd played in the mayhem the psycho was causing in Australia.

Nothing, not even the dorkishly delicious Lucas, would stand in my way.

Unsurprisingly, by the time I'd unlocked the house, brought in my limited supplies, started the generator, made sure the solar power system and batteries were functioning, and spent a few seconds staring ominously at the ridiculously small bed, Lucas appeared in the open doorway. The fact that I'd kept it open for him was a testimony to the generous mood I was in.

I wasn't sure if he agreed when he stepped into the wooden house, pausing in the small space, taking in the room.

His "No" pierced the air.

My grin was immediate. I turned slowly to face him, sadistic satisfaction worming its way through my veins from the way he stared wide-eyed at the bed in the tiny room off the sitting area.

"Problem?" I asked helpfully.

His gaze cut to mine. Tight-lipped, nostrils flaring, Lucas stared my way, the muscles in his cheeks tensing. When he didn't say anything, I grinned, the movement catching his attention as he zeroed in on my mouth before he glanced away.

Tempted to push him further but knowing better,

I reluctantly looked at the open doorway, saying, "As soon as that's closed and locked, I'll show you the rest."

The flash of relief in his gaze took me by surprise. Only because I didn't expect he was a man who gave much away.

I ignored the whisper of discomfort at the fact that the "rest" wasn't an extra bedroom. At least the underground setup would be impressive. While I hadn't seen it, all the syndicate's safe houses were kitted out with the same tech specs.

Door closed and locked, I headed to the small kitchenette. It was barely big enough for the stove, oven, and fridge, but it was more than enough for our needs. The outline on the floor was barely visible —likely invisible to humans—but I spotted it immediately.

I pressed the button hidden underneath the solitary wall cupboard. The floor hatch opened with a soft whoosh, revealing reinforced steel complete with a security panel. Much like with the first entrance, I completed the protocol, and the hatch slid open, revealing a ladder.

Lights flicked on, illuminating the space below as I headed down the few rungs, Lucas hot on my tail.

"Holy shit, what is this place?"

My lips twitched. I could probably count on one

hand how often Lucas cussed. Something stirred in my gut, my chest puffing out a little that revealing this setup to him earned such a reaction.

My feet found purchase on the concrete floor as I answered, "Just a safe location." I moved away to give Lucas room.

When he stepped off the final rung and glanced around, no doubt taking everything in, he asked, "Yours?" Curiosity pitched his voice a little high.

Rather than having to explain myself or the syndicate, I said, "Yes." I didn't owe Lucas anything, not even that response.

Uncertainty settled in his eyes as he stared my way. I turned my back to him. It was wise for him not to believe me—on this at least. "I'll switch on the mainframe. If you work on the Titan," I instructed, ignoring the heat trying to crawl up my neck. "Then we'll get started."

With my back to him as I turned on the mainframe, I heard Lucas move and a chair scrape across the floor. I waited, shoulders tense, for him to mention the computer setup we had. When he didn't and the first sound of the Titan whirring to life rang out, followed by the tapping of his fingers flying across the keys, I relaxed.

Why he didn't comment on the Titan being part of the elaborate setup—computer engineering he'd designed—I didn't know. After the way I'd been behaving, it would have been the perfect opportunity to give me shit for using his system. If the roles were reversed, I suspected I would have ribbed him something rotten.

Having completed the next set of security measures and booted up all the systems, including the monitors linked to the cameras and sensors located on the property, I sat on the second chair on the right-hand corner of the large setup. From here, if I glanced left, I could see both Lucas's screen and his side profile.

The tiniest of smirks, barely there and subtle, sat on his lips.

I rolled my eyes. "Shut the fuck up," I grumbled.

His brow immediately arched high, but he didn't look at me.

"Whatever. I can admit the Titan is the best system created." It didn't mean I'd congratulate him for being an annoying fucking tech genius. Screw that.

Hell, I hadn't—nor anyone else in the syndicate—needed to amend the machine either. There was no putting my own flair, my own signature on the computer.

There was no improving perfection.

His expression didn't shift even as he navigated through the system.

Relieved, I focussed on my own monitor. While I didn't really give a damn what he was working on, not communicating was a dick move. Especially if we ended up doubling up.

The urge to ask what he was concentrating on sat like acid in the back of my throat. I couldn't ask. Asking would be like needing instruction or permission or even a task. It had been a long time since I'd taken instruction or orders from anyone.

Sure, I took on jobs, had clients. But I picked and chose.

Fuck.

Knowing I'd chosen wrong, dead, dead wrong, when taking on the contract for Hornell—even though I hadn't known it was him, which simply made me more pissed off with myself—was a shitty reminder that I wasn't infallible.

Damn it.

I parted my lips, not sure I could form the words.

Did it make me an egotistical prick? Probably. More than that, I detested the wisp of vulnerability from having to communicate and open up—even if it was a simple exchange. Tension tightened my muscles. They bunched in my back. If I didn't get my shit together, I'd break out in a sweat.

No way did I want that scent in the air. Not with any supe in the vicinity, but especially not a vampire who could determine the tiniest semblance of distress. That prey-predator bullshit was built into their DNA.

Efficient words with barely any inflection drifted to me. "I'm tracing the breach into our location at Tamborine Mountain. I want to make sure that'll never happen again."

I swallowed back my scoff, confident that wouldn't happen here. *Fallible.* The word lodged in my brain. Sometimes my ego and cockiness were just and true. Fuck me impressed that I could keep my mouth shut… occasionally.

"After that, I'll touch base with the team, once I'm confident of the security," Lucas said.

The pulse in my neck throbbed, the muscles in my shoulders twitching involuntarily.

A barely there sigh escaped him, but there was no not hearing it. He continued, "I won't reveal our location."

If he expected a thank you, he'd be waiting a long time. I saved his arse and compromised one of the syndicate's safe houses. After this, the place would be dismantled, and a new location organised.

But I wasn't a complete twat.

Lucas sharing his intentions wasn't lost on me.

That he was smart enough to not attempt to give me an order didn't exactly endear him to me, but he hadn't been a dick, so there was that.

I offered, "Before we left, I was close to something. I'll check to see if that lead's come through from one of my contacts."

The sound of him gritting his teeth pulled my attention.

His strong jaw, which I detested looking at since it was all chiselled and smooth and had me wondering what his skin would feel like under my fingertips, flexed.

I dragged my gaze away and rolled my eyes. It was so much easier to be pissed off and annoyed at Lucas. Distraction could only lead to a whirlwind of chaos and shit.

"Murdock," I started, knowing full well Lucas wanted more than my cryptic "something." "I think we have something on Murdock. Enough leverage for Callen to take him in and get some truth and answers out of him."

A beat passed and another, but when he didn't push me for more, I relaxed, relieved he was letting me do my thing. My "thing" in this instance was doing whatever it took to get Hornell behind bars or, preferably, not breathing.

Only then would I be able to hop on a plane and get my arse home.

THIRTY HOURS, AND WHILE MURDOCK REMAINED IN custody, he hadn't broken. What we needed was greater leverage. But more than that, I needed sleep. I side-eyed Lucas.

He didn't look frazzled, exactly. I wasn't sure what it would take for him to look that way. He didn't appear like he was functioning at full capacity, either, though, but that was on him.

Last night, he'd refused to sleep, staying up and relentlessly researching and searching and following leads. While vampires didn't need as much rest as shifters and nowhere near as many hours as humans, they couldn't function on coffee and canned soup or plasma vials alone.

The need to tell him to pull his head out of his backside sat uncomfortably on my shoulders.

I shouldn't care. Wouldn't. Point-blank refused to. But what use was he to this mission if he didn't have the energy to do his job?

I cast another look. Shadows smudged the usually pale peachy whiteness under his eyes. While the lights weren't burning brightly, there was no hiding the pallor of his skin. An itch formed between my shoulder blades, and I tightened my jaw and glanced back at the screen.

The man had enough years on him, close to a hundred and fifty, that he could more than take care of himself. I flexed my jaw, trying to loosen the bunched muscles. Doing so tore a jaw-cracking yawn out of me.

Fuck it.

Five hours of sleep and I'd be good to get back to it.

Standing up from my workstation, I peered over at Lucas. He sat tall, ramrod straight with an intensely focussed gaze. A twitch directly below his right eye caught my attention. He was viscerally aware of my every move.

I turned away and walked over to the ladder, only to pause before lifting my foot to the first rung.

Damn the man.

I dropped my head, wishing like hell I could ignore Lucas, pretend I didn't see how close to exhaustion he was. It didn't matter that the past two days—more, really, when I considered the days in Tamborine—hadn't been spent physically racing around on a mission. The mental strain from staring at a screen and assessing data took its toll.

Through gritted teeth, I sighed before saying, "You need rest."

The slight scrape of the chair legs told me enough: he'd jumped. Fucking jumped when I'd spoken.

Shit, perhaps he wasn't as switched on as I thought.

Pissed off and determined, I turned to face Lucas. Our eyes connected, his wide. He was so spun out. If he didn't sleep soon, the dickhead would collapse.

Bloody vampires. I swore they were the most stubborn species alive, and considering bear shifters boasted many titles—stubborn and aggressive often being on top—that was saying something.

"You need to sleep," I gritted out, narrowing my gaze.

Another eye twitch and a firm, single shake of his head followed. "I'll rest later. I've managed to find the information on some tech recovered from one of Hornell's labs. The setup should carry active chips that could give us locations."

I stared hard, narrowing my gaze further. Not that it had any effect. Lucas didn't even flinch. But looking at him directly like this, at his faintly ashen skin, the slight hollowness of his cheekbones that looked more pronounced, it was hard not to wince. The man looked like shit.

An exaggeration? Sure. Lucas couldn't truly

appear as anything but annoyingly handsome, but this wasn't the put-together agent I was used to.

"When was the last time you drank?" I asked, my voice echoing in the dimly lit basement.

He clamped his jaw, and my eyes widened as a dull thump reached my ears.

His heartbeat.

In all my forty-five years, I could count on one hand how many times I'd heard a vampire's heartbeat.

The beats were slower than a sloth wading through molasses, quieter than the whisper of a breeze through autumn leaves. But there it was, unmistakable in its rhythm yet strangely erratic.

Surrounded by computers and equipment, the dim glow of monitors cast eerie shadows across Lucas's face, emphasising the lines of fatigue etched into his features. He pursed his lips.

"When was the last time you drank?" I repeated, my voice tinged with… *fuck*… concern as I studied him.

He hesitated, his gaze flickering away before meeting mine with a stubborn resolve. "It's been… a while," he admitted, his tone gruff with reluctance.

My heart sank as I realised the implications. Lucas was in trouble, and it was more serious than I had feared. I remembered the empty plasma vial I had seen discarded in the rubbish bin over a day ago. One vial for a vampire who required sustenance to survive was nowhere near sufficient.

Food helped provide some nourishment, but without blood, he'd be hurting.

"There were two more vials," he added quietly, almost as an afterthought. "But they... they broke somehow." A quick glance my way and he set his jaw, saying, "My emergency kit in the car had a week's supply. There wasn't room for it on the bike."

Ignoring his feeble snipe, I hooked on to his initial hesitation. The uncertainty I didn't ever expect to hear from him smacked me hard in the chest. I held back my wince at the need to rub at the annoying feeling lodged there.

Lucas not taking care of himself was a dick move. But then there was the damn feeling again, aching to protect him.

The whole thing was ridiculous. Lucas was not a vampire or an agent who needed protection.

Frustration mingled with concern as I processed his words while trying to ignore my reaction to him. Lucas could be infuriatingly stubborn, but my need to protect him outweighed any irritation.

I took the few steps needed to be in his space. "Come on," I said, my voice firm but insistent. "You need to rest."

Surprise flickered in his eyes, mingled with a hint of uncertainty.

"This won't put us behind. Sleep will help, right?"

"Yeah." A deep swallow followed. It appeared painful, and I wondered if his thirst burned.

"So let's rest, and then we'll figure out your feeding situation."

He nodded.

For a moment, I wasn't sure who was more astonished—him, for acquiescing to my request by standing, or me, for successfully persuading him.

Or the fact that I was doing this in the first place.

As we ascended the ladder, his steps slow and deliberate, I winced at the swell of conflicting emotions. Here was Agent Lucas, the epitome of togetherness and strength, leaning on me for support.

Warmth tried to creep across my skin and settle deep. Looking after him and him letting me care for him shouldn't be a big deal. I couldn't let it.

"Bed," I ordered, all tenderness gone.

What I needed was him out of my space so I could think. In this tiny wooden hut, that would be near impossible. The reminder of our proximity as he hesitated in the open doorway of the single bedroom was a stark reality check.

How the hell I got myself into these situations, I had no idea. It went to show how messed up everything was. We could have easily planned ahead, worked in some sort of shift system, but instead, the both of us worked until the point of exhaustion and—

I reached out, clamping my hand on Lucas's arm when he swayed.

He was worse than I thought.

Silently, I guided him to the bed and eased him to sit. My pointed look when we made eye contact was enough for him to blush and lift his legs.

Breath froze in my lungs at the pink in his cheeks. *Pink.* Had I ever seen a vampire blush before?

Forcing ice into my veins, I shook off my reaction, pushing aside the rare vulnerability evident in Lucas's features and the very fact that he not only let me but needed me to do this for him.

"Sleep," I ordered. With that, I spun on my heel and got the hell away from his pink cheeks, half-mast gaze, and scent. It was intoxicating, a mix of cedarwood, dark spices, and something uniquely him, sophisticated and mesmerising. The fragrance lingered in the air, wrapping around me like a forbidden embrace, making it difficult to think clearly.

I hated that I found it alluring, hated that it called

to something deep within me that I had buried long ago.

I fled the room, closing the door firmly behind me, as if that could shut out the scent and the troubling thoughts it provoked. Leaning against the door for a moment, I closed my eyes and took a deep breath, willing my heart to stop its frantic pounding.

I needed sleep, but the only bed was taken, and there was no way I was sharing with Lucas. The small settee in the corner was laughably inadequate, barely large enough to accommodate my big toe, let alone my entire body.

What I needed was to find a way to get Lucas much-needed blood, or at least plasma vials. Heading into town was not an option; it would likely reveal our location to those hunting us.

The only option would be to let him feed from me.

The thought sent a shiver down my spine—not just because of the danger but also because of what it would mean. Getting close to Lucas screamed peril, but at the same time, it stirred something protective and deeply buried within me. The man was too tempting for his own good, and he brought out the caretaker in me that I had long since pushed aside.

Terrified by the implications of falling for him, I pushed off from the door and began pacing the small room. What was my next course of action? Sleep was a distant hope, but necessity would drive me to find a solution. Lucas needed blood to recover, and I couldn't ignore that, no matter how much I wanted to avoid the intimacy it would entail.

I paused, glancing back at the closed door, my resolve hardening. Whatever it took, I would ensure we both survived this. Even if it meant confronting my own fears and desires head-on.

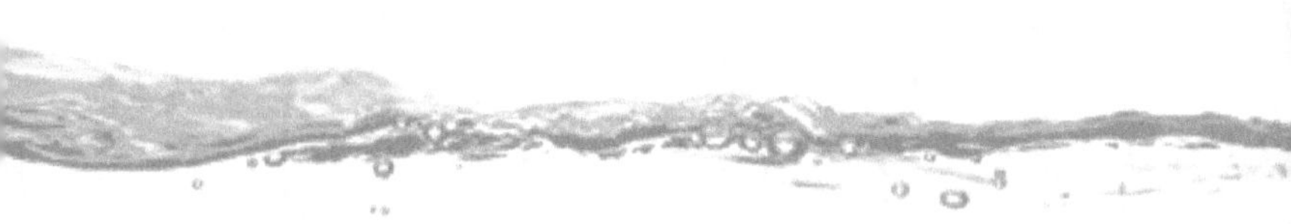

CHAPTER 3
LUCAS

THIRST SCRAMBLED MY BRAIN. GNAWING HUNGER singed my veins, clawing my stomach, a brutal reminder that I was a stubborn dick to have tried to ignore my reality.

Every decision I'd made went against the very fabric of my being.

I *wasn't* irresponsible. I *wasn't* a selfish idiot who made piss-poor decisions.

Having to tell Wilder the truth hurt more than it should have.

I gritted my molars and placed my forearm over my eyes, a heavy huff of air escaping me. Two hours holed up in the bedroom and I'd barely managed a minute of rest.

Who knew my ego would be my downfall? If my team could see me now, I liked to think they wouldn't recognise me. My pride was putting the mission—and me—in danger. What on earth had I been thinking?

Deep brown eyes bleeding with concern filled my vision, forming behind my closed eyes. Wilder. Thoughts about the bear who delighted in vexing me, who took great effort to rattle me and argue at every turn—that was if he wasn't freezing me out— battled for space in my mind.

Somehow, he'd found a crack in the armour I'd spent over three decades constructing. Without a crowbar in sight, he'd pried it open and found room for himself—so much so, it took everything in me not to react or respond.

What a rubbish job I'd made of that.

Reacting at every turn, I'd taken it so far that he'd all but tucked me into bed. Showed a sliver of compassion that attempted to pivot what I thought I knew about him. If only I could stop fixating on how he'd stepped in, somehow managed to get me to admit the truth, and then *cared* for me, I would embrace the fire licking through my veins to push me into unconsciousness.

It was impossible. Even the tightening of my skin and the razor-sharp stings as I swallowed couldn't shake him free from my mind.

Sleep wouldn't truly stop my hunger, but it had been a long time since I'd felt this level of exhaustion.

A hollow laugh bubbled out of me, and I pulled my arm away, letting the dulling light press against my shut eyelids. I'd got myself into this situation. Only I could get myself out of it.

Forcing my eyes open, I stared up at the ceiling. The rough-cut wood had been painted at one point but was in desperate need of a fresh coat. A little like me. A humourless snort escaped, and I shook my head. I was losing the plot if I was comparing myself to something needing a new layer of paint.

That I'd let my situation get this bad hollowed out my smile.

I knew better. Should have *done* better.

It was one thing being in the city and living and breathing work. A place where someone else took care of ensuring a weekly delivery of food and plasma vials were stocked. My house wasn't much better than this.

I glanced around, taking in the basic furnishings and bare walls.

Yeah, not so dissimilar at all.

Which was a complete exaggeration, since my converted warehouse was kitted out in the highest security and boasted a control centre to a higher spec than that at the unit's base. But it was behind the closed doors to my living quarters that told a different story.

Sure, there was a guest space that was maintained but rarely used. The last time was a couple of years back when used as a safe house. But still, it was tidy and well-stocked in case it should be needed again.

Unlike my own private space.

A fresh stab blade of pain stabbed my stomach. This wasn't a hunger that could be satisfied by food.

Fucking pathetic.

The words sliced through me, not my own, instead a cruel memory, but absolutely fitting.

Why the hell would the government let me run a covert department when I couldn't even feed myself? A sneer lifted my lips.

I knew why.

Of course I did.

Yes, I was incredible at my job. That wasn't simply my ego talking. But it was more than that. Not a single person knew what a shitshow everything else was.

The door creaked open. I snapped my eyes in its direction, my traitorous heart stumbling. It felt strange that it was making any sound or quick movement at all.

The heady scent of pine trees and cedarwood filled the air, mingling with the faint hint of earth and musk that seemed to cling to Wilder. It was a scent that spoke of wild forests and untamed wilderness, something primal and powerful.

I shouldn't like it, and I definitely shouldn't take comfort in it, but he'd cared for me. Looked after me. I hated to remember the last time I'd allowed that to happen, but somehow, Wilder had known that I couldn't pull myself away from my mission in the basement, too determined and stubborn to admit there was a problem.

Wilder stood in the doorway, his large form nearly filling the frame. His presence was imposing, yet there was a gentleness in the way he held himself. His dark brown eyes, deep and thoughtful, locked onto mine with an intensity that made my breath catch. The thick, bushy beard that framed his strong jawline was as wild as the rest of him, adding to the ruggedness that made it difficult to glance away.

There was a crackling energy between us, as if the very air was charged with a current that neither of us could ignore. The hairs on the back of my neck stood on end while my skin tingled with awareness. His eyes held a question, concern mingled with some-thing else I couldn't quite place.

"Is something wrong?" I asked, breaking the silence that had stretched between us, my voice barely above a whisper.

Wordlessly, he stepped into the small room, his form filling the space so completely that my breath froze in my lungs.

"You need to feed."

The "No shit, Sherlock" I was about to unleash got trapped in my throat when he narrowed his gaze, just daring me to respond in a way that would piss him off. Oh so tempting, but as my energy whooshed out of me with every slow breath, I instead let my head fall to the pillow.

"Once I've slept, I'll figure something out. Arrange a safe drop-off." It was the only option.

I couldn't go into town. Too many surveillance cameras existed in every town and city, even those as remote as this place. It would be a matter of arranging a deal with someone who could be trusted and somewhere without prying eyes.

"You need to feed," he repeated, his voice closer. It was the creak of the old floorboard under his solid form that had me snapping my attention back to him, though.

Wide-eyed, I stared at him. Standing close to the bed, he towered over me. That should not have been as triggering to my dick as it was. But hell if his size and the stubborn set of his jaw didn't unfurl desire in my gut.

"I heard you the first time, and I'm not disagreeing." I held my voice tight, limbs taut under his scrutiny. "I also said I'll figure something out when I've slept."

A silent beat followed before he arched his brow. "So after sleep, you'll miraculously feel better and be functioning at full capacity, or at least enough to get your brain cells working to organise something that you could have done the moment you discovered you had one vial to last you."

"Fuck you." The words punched out of me. That he was right was neither here nor there. The arsehole needed to back off. "And close the door on your way out."

Ignoring me, he stepped even closer. A smile that was a hundred percent satisfaction formed.

Tension thrummed through me at the expression. Despite the past few years focussing on understanding and manipulating technology, I'd read people for decades. My switch in expertise, no longer being in the field, didn't mean I'd lost my ability to understand what that kick of his lips meant.

Slowly, so painfully slowly, Wilder tugged up the long sleeves of the soft black band tee he wore.

"The hell do you think you're doing?" I dropped my gaze to his exposed forearms, zeroing in on a meaty vein throbbing close to his skin.

I couldn't close my eyes. I refused to let him know

how much he was affecting me. *The thirst*, I quickly tagged on to my thoughts. The tightness in my gut, the itch in my gums, it was all because I was so damn thirsty, and it had nothing to do with his burly arms or the overlay of iron-infused ink decorating his skin that made it practically impossible to tear my gaze away.

The tattoos must have been burnt and seared when he'd had the artwork inked—the only way, since his shifter genes would have dissolved normal ink almost as fast as the tattooist could have worked it into his skin.

Look away, look away, look away.

My breath hitched when he paused within touching distance. The traitorous sound did what my brain had been unable to do—pulled me away from eating up the expanse of his skin. I glanced up, and our eyes locked. While his smirk remained, intensity shone in his gaze, something dark and dangerous.

His pupils flickered, dancing over my face, and I held still, wondering at the uncertainty I saw in their depths.

Wilder had been as cocky as a kangaroo in a boxing ring—all huge and dominant and full of over-inflated ego. Now? Now, not so much. A battle, a war, a doubt was being waged.

His smile slipped, and his hand moved quickly,

but rather than reaching for me, it moved around his back, reappearing with a plasma vial. "Here." Gravel thickened his voice, and I had barely a second to catch the vial he threw my way.

Then he was retreating, turning, and racing out of the room like demons were chasing him. Though I suspected it was disbelief.

'Cause heck if that wasn't exactly what worked through my system as I sat, clutching the plasma vial, a flurry of questions buzzing through my brain.

He'd found a vial.

Had this been here the whole time, or had he managed to track it down somehow?

While I hadn't heard him leave, my senses were not as they should be, my hunger distr—

Pain cramped my stomach. I winced, immediately uncorking the small vial. The scent of synthesised blood clogged my sinuses, my teeth elongating despite not needing them. I brought the tube to my lips, angled my head, and swallowed the contents.

The relief was instant as the blood, barely more than 50 mL, slithered down my throat, but the effects were immediate.

The triple-strength fluid wasn't meant to be savoured. Not truly. It was a means to an end, an emergency tool to stop vampires from feeding on humans and shifters alike—even though the differences between the effects on the two species were greatly different.

Though it tasted nothing like the real thing and was even leagues below the taste of the larger elite vials that were part of my home delivery service, the outcome was almost the same. And fast.

Relief bloomed in my stomach as my head cleared and my pain dissipated, barely leaving a shadow of discomfort behind. I collapsed back on the mattress, a content sigh escaping. Gratitude lodged in my chest.

Wilder had made this happen and sourced a vial to help me.

I turned over onto my side and peered out the window into the darkening sky. Stars flickered up high, like scattered diamonds against a velvety expanse. The crescent moon hung low, casting a gentle glow over the world below. The peacefulness of the night wrapped around me, a comforting blanket that eased the remnants of tension from my body.

For the first time in days, I felt a true sense of calm. How, I was unsure. How could I feel calm when not in my own space and relying on a man I struggled to trust?

I expelled a breath, more for its soothing ability than necessity. The serenity of the night sky seemed to seep into my very bones, allowing me to drift closer to sleep. My heartbeat slowed, matching the rhythmic pulse of the universe outside.

Yet, as I lay there, on the edge of slumber, a thought wormed its way into my mind. Wilder had always been a wild card, an unknown in my carefully structured world, but maybe there was more to him than met the eye. There was a depth to his actions, a layer of intention that hinted at something beyond the brash exterior.

Perhaps Wilder was more than he appeared to be —a complexity hidden beneath the bravado.

With that thought lingering, I let the tranquillity of the night lull me into a deep, restful sleep.

I MANAGED TO TIPTOE PAST WILDER SLEEPING awkwardly on the couch, his body much larger than the tiny frame, guilt urging me to get back to the mission. The sooner we completed it, the sooner he could leave.

That the thought left a sour taste in my mouth was something I doggedly ignored.

As the hum of computers settled around me, I found my rhythm, alternating between touching base with the team and following leads.

For three hours, I followed the trail needed to

finally get some answers from Murdock. While doing a deep dive into his cloud and his trash, which he foolishly expected to be destroyed, I paused at the innocuous name on a secured document.

While the title *Morning Meeting* shouldn't ring alarm bells that it was a secure document, considering his position as assistant defence minister, the fact that I found it so easily was concerning. Government officials followed strict protocols when deleting files, making the kind of lurking I was currently doing impossible. The ease with which I found the note meant that he'd trashed it carelessly and not through the official government channels.

A creak alerted me to Wilder's movements.

I fought against my reaction, the tenderness trying to take hold and clamber to the surface when I thought about his care and attention and the way the deep lines between his brows had disappeared when he'd been fast asleep on the uncomfortable sofa.

I worked my way into the document, forcing my shoulders to relax when Wilder's feet touched the concrete floor and he stepped fully into the basement.

"What do you have?" he rumbled, tiredness still obvious in his sleep-rough voice.

The gravel tried to wrap around me, make the

small hairs on my arms stand on end. No way would I let that happen.

Instead, I focussed on his question, embracing my relief that we were concentrating on work. The task I could handle. Talking about anything else right now, I couldn't. Not without saying, thinking, or possibly doing something I shouldn't.

"A note in Murdock's cloud," I offered.

The heady scent of pine drew nearer, and when Wilder reached my side, I cast a brief look his way. Eyes on the screen, Wilder appeared engrossed and not at all bothered by the kindness he'd shown me.

It helped me turn my attention back to the screen.

"Hasn't that already been checked?"

"Not the Shadow Stratus."

A subtle movement from Wilder told me his reaction had been the same as mine.

"What the hell is the assistant defence minister doing with access to the Shadow?"

"Let's find out." I weaved through the security system in place with worrying ease considering I absolutely wasn't the only person capable of doing such a thing. Anything in here that put our country at risk could easily be placed in the hands of someone with nefarious intentions. And that the information could be accessed via the Shadow—an illegal cloud synonymous with all that was depraved in our world—yeah, I had a feeling I wasn't going to like what I found.

"What the fuck?" Dark indignation sharpened Wilder's words.

Speechless, I shook my head as I scrolled through the notes, pausing on the embedded images. Disgust slithered across my skin, and the pit of dread solidified once the vastness of what we'd uncovered registered.

"This is…." Words escaped me.

Wilder leaned in closer, his voice dropping to a whisper. "They're using Hornell's illegal technology. Look at this." He pointed at a section detailing experimental weapons—viciously effective but grotesque in their construction and use.

"And here," I added, scrolling further. "Cruel experiments involving shifters. They're not just capturing them—they're weaponising them." Images of caged shifters, their bodies altered and augmented with technology, filled the screen.

"These notes detail direct orders from Murdock," Wilder said, his tone grave. "He's not just in cahoots with Hornell; he's a key player. A branch of the Australian Defence Ministry is funding and utilising this technology."

"Which means," I added, my heart pounding, "we have the leverage we need. If this gets out, it would be a national scandal. The Defence Ministry would be crippled, and Murdock's career would be over." Hell, he'd be looking at life imprisonment.

"But more importantly," Wilder continued, "we can use this to force Murdock's hand. He'll have no choice but to tell us where Hornell is. His entire operation would collapse under the weight of this information."

I nodded, a plan forming in my mind. "We need to secure this data and confront Murdock. If we can get him to reveal Hornell's location, we can shut this entire operation down and finally get to Hornell."

"Agreed," Wilder said, his jaw set with determination. "But we need to move quickly. If Hornell gets wind that we have this, he'll try to bury it—and us."

With a final look at the screen, the gravity of our discovery washed over me. The fate of countless lives, human and shifter alike, hung in the balance. We had to act, and fast.

I would have scoffed at that if my lungs hadn't constricted. It wasn't like we didn't already know how important it was to take Hornell down.

But the depth of the government's involvement was unthinkable.

Immediately, I reached out to Callen.

He opened with "The line's secure. Director Durrant is with me."

I startled at Wilder's arm reaching over me. Before I could question him, he hit Mute. I glanced at him, my brows high.

"You sure you can trust her?"

He was referring to the SICB director.

"Yes." No hesitation existed when it came to Durrant. Every step of the way, she'd supported the unit. Even before I'd joined, she'd stamped out corruption in the division. I trusted her implicitly; so did Callen and Thatch.

Wilder studied me, and our gazes connected, his searching. He nodded once, unmuted us, and eased back.

He believed me. Trusted I knew my team. I stopped my breath from stuttering out of me, aware Callen was waiting for my response.

"I'm sending you something. Make sure the two of you are somewhere secure."

"We already are," Durrant answered. "I have a feeling we're not going to like what you send."

I sent the encrypted file. "You could say that, Director. But it's also what we need to change everything and finally put this to bed."

"We need everything you have. Murdock's not budging," Callen said.

"Not even to your more intriguing questioning

methods?" My lips twitched despite the seriousness of the situation.

Callen snorted. "I don't think anyone here in the capital would appreciate my more creative interviewing methods."

I angled a look at Wilder, who sat beside me. Curiosity coloured his expression. Once again, my lips twitched, and his eyes darted to them. Glancing away, I responded, "I can only imagine."

Callen's tone turned serious. "Okay, we've got it. Opening it now."

One beat. A second.

"The ever-loving fuck!" Callen exploded.

Durrant cut in. "I won't insult you by asking the validity of this intel." The strain was evident in her voice.

"I appreciate that." We'd known each other for my entire life. She was the reason I joined the SICB in the first place.

"I'm going to send you a list," she continued. "We're going to have to tread carefully, as this is going to cause ripples I'm not sure any of us are fully prepared for."

"I hear you, Director."

"Have I ever told you the story about trapping a viper in the corner of a room?" Tight amusement strained her words.

"Not sure you have."

"Hmm… maybe another time over a bottle of Château Lafite Rothschild."

Wilder stirred at my side, no doubt wondering about my familiarity with Durrant.

"For now, just know that a whole nest of cornered snakes can prove deadly," Director Durrant warned, her voice lowering to a solemn tone. "And we're about to step into that room."

"Understood." I comprehended the gravity of her analogy with the weight of experience. A nest of cornered government officials, desperate and threatened, could strike out unpredictably, potentially endangering anyone in their path.

"We're going to move Murdock somewhere off-grid now. I'll get Kent to set something up. As soon as you receive my list, you'll know what to do."

"We've got this, Director."

There was a pause before she spoke again—whether at the use of "we" or a recollection of all we'd been through, I didn't know. "You need to make sure you and the team are truly underground," she continued, her words laden with caution. "And, Mathew, watch your back." Her tone softened. "You know that in a viper's den, danger lurks in every shadow."

Her warning sent a shiver down my spine,

reminding me of the perilous game we were about to play.

The communication cut off, the quiet feeling heavy after the exchange.

"She's worried about you." Wilder's deep voice rumbled across my skin. "You know her outside of work."

An absolute statement.

"She used to be my mother's best friend." The words fell free, unbidden. I slammed my lips together, confusion furrowing my brow as I wondered why on earth I'd shared as much with him. Nobody beyond Kent and Callen knew about our connection.

Not that it was disastrous if anyone knew.

I'd had decades to prove my worth.

What I didn't plan on was sharing so much of myself with anyone, let alone the English bear who'd done nothing but make my fangs itch since the moment I'd laid eyes on him.

An alert drew my attention. I grabbed on to the need to focus on the imminent threat rather than the discomfort of oversharing with Wilder.

"It's Durrant's list," I said unnecessarily, but the need to cut through the tension urged me on. "I know most of these names." Scrolling the list, I read through each, understanding immediately without instruction what Durrant's play was.

"You know them personally…?"

I shook my head. "Only some, but I recognise the majority of names as individuals Durrant trusts."

"She wants you to organise the troops and get ready for a takedown."

I glanced at Wilder, who turned to make eye contact. That he so quickly caught up without explanation wasn't so much a surprise as it was intriguing. There was so much about this man I didn't know.

What I did know was, Hart trusted him—despite the confrontation before we left Sydney—and Smythe trusted his boyfriend implicitly. Wilder had also gone above and beyond to help my unit.

"Where did you get the vials from?" There was a whole stack waiting in the kitchen when I'd resurfaced after sleeping.

By the flicker of a reaction before he locked himself down, it was clear he was as surprised as I was that I was asking him this question, not only at all, but now. Were there more pressing matters? Definitely. But I needed to know, my instinct in the driving seat and ready to push him on this if necessary.

Not that it was needed, as after a quiet study of

my face, he said, "I drove forty klicks west to a drop-off point."

"You were able to arrange something so soon?" Even as I asked, I felt foolish. He'd clearly arranged something quickly.

Rather than calling me out, he bobbed his head. "I called in a favour."

I quirked my brow, wondering just how extensive his reach was that he could organise everything while being thousands of kilometres away from home. We weren't exactly close to a major city either.

I settled on "Thank you."

A flicker of discomfort seemed to shroud him, his gaze darting away briefly before he peered back at me. His shrug was nowhere near as casual as I assumed he intended as he said, "I needed you on your game. The sooner we clean up this clusterfuck, the sooner I can jump on a plane."

While the bite in his tone was gone, I read his not-so-subtle request for me to let it go and move on.

That I could absolutely do.

Immediately, I set to work on the names, considering the best way to reach out to the Collection. The individuals spanned from various units within the SICB to Canberra to the Air Force to different military branches—several of which were overseas.

One name jumped out at me. I paused, taking it in.

"Who's Valeria Blackthorn?"

I closed my eyes, my fingers tingling, urging me to wipe a frustrated hand over my face. If I'd been by myself, it was what I would have done. I probably would have smashed the computer across the wall too.

"Valeria Blackthorn," Wilder repeated, and I could practically hear his brain ticking over, trying to think where he knew that name. "I've heard of *Vance* Blackthorn. He's the agent who took down the Lancelot Project over a decade ago. Are they related?"

I winced, wanting Valeria far, far away from this mission. Not that she wasn't beyond capable. "Vance… *her* name is Valeria now."

"Huh, no shit." His brows dipped. "Isn't she retired or something?"

A fizzle of warmth bloomed that Wilder immediately grasped the correct pronoun. Not that it was hard to grasp. "Or something," I answered. "That you think that is exactly what they want you to believe. She's very much active but rarely returns home." Which I knew I was responsible for, but hell if I didn't miss her with every fibre of my being.

"Oh shit, you *know her* know her."

I jerked quickly to face him, horror drifting over me. He jolted back in surprise at my expression.

"O-kay," he said slowly, questions filling his gaze. "So *not* like that then. My bad." As he spoke, his shoulders relaxed a fraction and something close to relief flickered in the depths of his eyes. "So, Valeria Blackthorn," he prompted, expectation directed my way.

I swore this man pushed buttons I didn't know I had. Worse than that, he managed to pry from me not only secrets but parts of myself I rarely offered to anyone. It had been decades since the last time.

There was no escaping the truth. Not when we were stuck in a remote cabin in the middle of nowhere. As soon as I made contact with Valeria, he'd know anyway.

"My daughter," I answered. "Valeria Blackthorn is my daughter."

CHAPTER 4
WILDER

You could have knocked me down with a feather and proceeded to bash me around with it for a little while.

His daughter?

How the fuck didn't I know that?

Come to think of it, how was nobody aware of this information? And if they were, his circle was more tight-lipped than a monk at a mime convention. Impressive. It also said a lot about those in his confidence.

Awareness pulsed inside me. Was I now in his confidence?

My skin itched. I wasn't sure how to process that possibility.

"Shit, right...." I bobbed my head once before catching up with not only everything he'd said but his whole tone. "And you don't want her involved, or you don't want her here?"

For the second time since we'd met, vulnerability etched across his features. Lucas sagged in his chair, appearing more human than I'd ever expected him to look. Uncertainty made my skin itched even more when I noticed the discomfort seeping into his gaze.

Making eye contact, he shook his head, saying, "I haven't seen her for eight years, not for lack of trying."

I held back my surprise. Lucas seemed like the kind of man to hold close to family, to those he cared about and loved.

"She's still working for the government in a capacity that I'm not a hundred percent sure about. Even if I was, I wouldn't be able to discuss it."

"Is that why you haven't seen her?" I prompted, curiosity to discover more about Lucas urging me on. Was he pissed at her, or was she pissed at him?

"Partially. I'm not sure where she's been based or what her role has been. But the last time we saw each other, I wasn't her favourite person."

I frowned. I couldn't imagine Lucas being the kind of man to take issue with his daughter's identity.

"And whatever you're thinking," he started, a frown appearing, "that's not it. I love my daughter, fiercely and completely. She's incredible and fantastic at her job and always has been."

While it was a relief to know Lucas wasn't a prick, I was still nosey as hell. "So, what did you do to piss her off?"

A humourless huff escaped him. "What didn't I do?"

I winced, a sympathetic smile forming. "That bad, huh?"

"Only if you think interfering with an investigation and blowing your daughter's cover after discovering an imminent threat to her and then going above her head to get her pulled is a bad thing."

"Ouch." I scrunched my face. "You went above her head? Yeah, that'll do it."

A shadow of guilt passed over his face. Interesting.

"And what else?" No way was that the only thing. From his reaction alone, it was obvious there was more to the tale. Add in the "retirement" story, and I suspected I was right.

"Just some shit I wish I could take back and had been honest about." He shook his head and sat upright, turning his focus away from me and back to the screen.

Disappointment weighed on my chest that he'd

held back. Foolish of me for sure. We didn't owe each other anything.

"Okay, let's work on this list."

Lucas effectively shut down the discussion with his instruction, and with no choice but to let it go, we worked side by side, at times relying on more ingenious ways to reach out to the contacts, especially those not contactable by more official channels.

Not that anything we were doing was exactly "official" considering I wasn't "officially" in the country and Lucas had a warrant out for questioning.

We needed to stay under the radar.

Based on what we'd discovered and Durrant's plan, if word got out about the takedown we had planned, it would destroy any chance at shutting down Murdock's corruption and work with Hornell. Hornell would be deeper in the wind before we got a breath away. The involvement of Jefferson, the other government official, still wasn't clear. But considering what we'd learnt about Murdock, we were treating him as a key player in the conspiracy taking place.

We'd since heard from Durrant, letting us know Jefferson had been taken into custody. Once again unofficially and to a covert ops site.

By the time we'd reached the bottom of Durrant's list, with me taking on the job to contact Agent

Lucas's daughter, grit scratched my eyes and my stomach rumbled.

"That's our cue to break."

I threw a surprised glance at Lucas, struggling to get a grip on this strange amity we now had. It was an unspoken truce of sorts. "I could eat," I offered. The tension around his eyes held me back from lapsing into my usual sarcastic comeback. "Do you need food or a vial?"

A moment's hesitation preceded his "Both."

I bobbed my head, wondering what the final straw was that had pushed us to be civilised. I wasn't sure how I felt, but I could admit that Lucas pressed my buttons. Perhaps that he wasn't quite the rule follower I'd thought he was had something to do with it. That and he'd screwed up with the whole blood thing but hadn't backtracked or shifted blame.

I stood. "I'll head up and make something." The man needed to eat and keep up his energy. Six hours had passed since our talk with Durrant.

"You don't nee—"

"What *I* need is for you to finish up here and be upstairs in twenty-five." I stared him down, expecting defiance. What I discovered made my heart trip over itself. Intensity filled his gaze while his shoulders loosened so minutely that I would have likely missed it if I hadn't been aware of his every move since we'd been locked away in this cabin together.

"After that, we need to take a ride." The offer was out there before I'd truly formed the thought or the idea, but fuck if the memory of his loud, carefree laugh when on the back of the motorbike didn't keep revisiting me. He needed that again. Needed a break. Hell, so did I, especially because, by this time tomorrow, shit would have hit the fan and there would be no resting at all.

And since I'd told him his daughter would be at the rendezvous point in twelve hours, he needed a change of scenery even more.

With my chin jutted in challenge, I waited a beat for him to argue. When he didn't, I nodded and turned, working hard to contain the squirm of satisfaction wriggling in my gut. I liked that he was letting me do this for him a little too much.

Closing the hatch behind me, I stepped into the kitchen area. Confident the basement was sealed and soundproof, I released a loud "Fuck!" I swiped a hand over my face.

The hell was I playing at?

Fire. It was the only answer.

Less than a handful of days of knowing the uptight vampire and I was spiralling. I clasped the kitchen countertop and dropped my head with a snort.

Nothing about the increasing urge to care for Lucas made sense. Sure, the desire to fuck him had been there from the moment I set eyes on him. He was sexy as hell. But looking after him… a man who, on the surface, seemed to have his shit together…? That there was the quandary.

The leader, the man in charge of the ITU, was not completely who he said he was.

Did he lie even to himself?

I glanced at the sealed hatch in the floor, visualising the vampire focussed intently on his computer screen. Lucas definitely held a part of himself back. I wondered if that was from everyone, if he trusted anyone enough to show them all the parts of himself.

Who are you really, Mathew Lucas?

The question was dangerous, especially as the desire to unravel him and discover his truth was a force I couldn't ignore.

"Fuck it all to hell." I rolled my eyes and set about making some food.

Fate had a wicked sense of humour. I swore she was laughing her arse off at me… at the promises I'd made myself over the years.

Criminal, vigilante, and a whole bunch of other descriptors assigned to me should have had me jumping on the first flight out of here days ago. Me joining forces with any government agent didn't make a lick of sense. Hell, it went against the grain, the very fibre of my being.

I tugged open the fridge door, eyeing the thawed steak I'd pulled out of the stocked underground freezer a few hours ago. There was something to be said about the intense heat in Australia. That would do nicely, and I suspected Lucas liked his rare too.

I set about seasoning the steak and tried to contain my thoughts on the mission and what we needed to do before Durrant's contacts gathered. They'd be in four different locations, and it would take some precision to navigate—not just because of the scope of the task, but because there were a lot of players in the mix.

When working in the cyber unit back home years ago, dealing with in-house politics had been enough to drive me to distraction. It was working with external agencies, though, that always gave me a headache and pulled my temper to the surface.

My patience for dealing with bullshit had been fried long ago, so just the thought of juggling egos brought a growl to the surface. The sizzle of the steak in the frying pan rose and drowned out my growl.

Lucas could handle it, though. I nudged the cooking steak. While I'd only witnessed his efficiency and diplomacy on a small scale, I had little doubt he could handle any number of supes and agents that needed wrangling.

A soft whoosh alerted me to the hatch opening.

After flipping the steak, I angled a look over my shoulder. Lucas emerged, his handsome face and bright eyes hiding the tiredness I knew he tried to conceal. It didn't matter that vampires didn't require a great amount of sleep. The pressure of the mission combined with his thirty-six hours of shit decision-making had hit him hard.

Despite the exhaustion ebbing off him, he remained distractingly sexy.

"You want salad?" I asked, my voice gruff. It always was when I raked my gaze over Lucas for longer than I should.

His gaze drifted to the frying pan, softening a moment before returning to meet mine. "I can put together one for you."

My lips hitched up. "Not much nutrition in salad for you, huh?"

He stepped closer, his shoulders relaxed. "Not enough to make me eat it. A carrot's great for my fangs, though."

My brows shot high, and a huff of laughter spilled from me. His mouth twitched, amusement outshining the slight shadows present on his face a moment ago.

"The man's got jokes. Fuck me and stop the press."

He flipped me off as he walked towards the fridge, and I turned back to the frying pan, hiding the huge grin refusing to leave me. It wasn't like he was even *that* funny, but slowly breaking down the strait-laced exterior he'd drowned in starch was impacting my defences.

"Are you a heathen who likes cucumber?"

"It all depends if that's a euphemism or not," I shot back. It was too late to clamp my mouth shut.

"Seriously…?" He dragged the word out. I side-eyed him, barely keeping my amusement in check when he shook his head, saying, "For a grumpy arse-hole, you flirt like you're getting paid by the hour."

"Hey, don't underestimate the power of being ridiculously good at it," I retorted, raising an eyebrow. "It's an art form. Picasso had his blue period; I have my flirtation period."

He snorted, his scowl cracking just a bit. "Period? Is that what you were doing with Hart?" His brows shot high as soon as he asked.

I was right there with him, surprised as hell he'd mentioned a brief exchange from over a week ago.

A slow smile slid onto my lips as I switched off

the burner and angled fully to face him. He stood there as if someone had hit Pause on the remote of life, his expression resembling that of a squirrel who just realised it forgot where it buried its nuts.

"Hart and I go way back," I started, feeling the urge to make my position clear. "It's called keeping people on their toes, Lucas. I thrive on unpredictability."

"Or you just enjoy the attention," he grumbled, breaking eye contact. A little too diligently, he worked on putting the salad together.

No way was I not answering. A little push and I was sure I'd be able to see another blush. "Who doesn't? Besides, your idea of flirting is what, asking if someone likes spreadsheets?"

Lame.

Admittedly it wasn't my best comeback, but his huff of laughter was a win.

"Hey, spreadsheets can be sexy."

Heat gathered low in my stomach. This conversation was beyond ridiculous and absolutely pointless. Regardless, he'd fired back, amusement blurring the edges of his words.

"Sure, if you're trying to woo an accountant. Which, knowing you, wouldn't surprise me."

"And what's wrong with accountants?"

A sting of something uncomfortable flushed

inside my chest. He was all jest, but the thought of him with anyone, let alone a boring fuck…. Yeah, no, I didn't like it one bit. "Nothing, if you're into balance sheets and… excitement that only happens at tax season."

He chuckled, shaking his head. "You're impossible."

I laid it on thick. "Impossibly charming, you mean."

"Keep telling yourself that," he said, rolling his eyes. "Maybe one day you'll believe it."

"Believe it? Lucas, honey, I live it," I declared. "Now, salad… I'd hate for HR to think we're having too much fun."

He snorted and once again shook his head, the ghost of a smile playing on his lips. "Hell, the last time I reported to HR was when you were a cub." He arched his brow, and fuck if the way his gaze roamed my body didn't make my dick take notice. "And if I did, like hell I'd be reporting anything that happened while we were here."

The implications almost had me swallowing my tongue. "Damn…," I managed, "like a whole 'what happens in Vegas stays in Vegas' scenario?" 'Cause, seriously, I could totally get on board with that. Pretend that all my issues and promises to not get up close and personal with Lucas didn't exist *just* while we were here…? Fuck yes. My interested cock turned rigid.

"That's not what I—"

"It's not?" I said as I took a step in his direction.

His eyes widened, his head angling back as I took one step closer.

He didn't speak, but neither was he stepping away.

"So, what *did* you mean?" Once we were practically chest to chest, I breathed him in. How the man smelled of cinnamon and rich earth, I had no clue. The combination should have been bizarre and unappealing.

It wasn't. Not when drifting off Lucas with his barely there breaths. While still slow compared to mine—a shifter's—they were much faster than normal for a vampire.

He dipped his chin, and I lost his gaze. I missed the defiance, the certainty I usually saw immediately.

What I should have done was step away, let him go. We both knew this was beyond foolish. But my gravelly "Look at me" escaped anyway.

The moment he lifted his gaze and we made eye contact, I was done for. That quiet, rare vulnerability I'd previously caught glimpses of lay on display. It was impossible not to eat it up, grab hold and take it, lap it up, and have ownership.

"Give me your hands."

The hesitation lasted a split second before he held them out. I angled to give him room, then took hold of his cool palms. On contact, his gaze wavered. Lucas following orders was a beautiful thing.

I manoeuvred his hands deliberately, slowly, and placed them around my neck. Wide-eyed, he stared at me. I suspected he was struggling to believe he was going along with this.

Not wanting to lose him, especially not with the way his eyes glazed a little, I dropped my voice, instructing, "Hold on."

He did.

My cock punched against my jeans.

So fucking beautiful. Responsive.

Cupping his backside, I lifted him as I ordered, "Kiss me," while encouraging him to wrap his legs around my waist before I settled him on the small table.

One beat. Two.

"Now, Matt. Kiss me."

A fresh shine appeared in his eyes, a slight sag in his shoulders as he expelled a breath. His lips touched mine, ice to my fire, and fuck if the contact didn't make my blood sizzle.

Any moment of hesitation Lucas may have had dissipated as I deepened the kiss. He responded eagerly, his hands tightening around my neck, drawing me closer. I guided the kiss, my hunger driving me to capture every taste and the low moans drifting between us. I lapped at him, opened wider, encouraged him to delve deeper.

Our kisses turned feverish, intense to the point of overwhelming.

Desperation fuelled my actions, a primal need urging me on. With each kiss, each touch, I held him tighter, holding him still. Letting him continue to grind against me would have had me coming in an embarrassingly short amount of time. I'd need his cock down my throat and his cum in my belly as he begged for everything before I was willing to let go.

His hands tightened on my neck, anchoring us. Me to him.

"I need…," he said with a gasp, pulling his lips from mine.

"What? Tell me."

The flush I'd been waiting for painted his cheeks. My fingers squeezed his backside on reflex. What would he look like spread naked under me, his usually pale skin pink with desperation and desire?

Fuck. I needed to know. Craved to lick every inch of him as he came apart with my fingers and tongue. Wanted him to bounce on my cock until he lost all sense of composure, every semblance of who he was.

"You." He gulped, his eyes shining with recklessness that I was determined to commit to memory.

I waited him out, brows arched in question, sure there was more. Though him having me was already a done deal.

"You," he repeated, the pink deepening to a scorching red as he admitted, "taking the lead... control."

Fuck me dead.

My mouth latched onto his with a fierceness that I knew he could handle. Our tongues tangled, the kiss turning possessive as I held his body, my dick pressing against his stomach. If he needed to give up control, wanted me to take over everything, I was here for it all.

My blood sang at the thought, his gasps and whimpers so at odds with the confident, self-assured vampire I knew. Every sound called to me.

Instinctively, I latched onto his throat, my grip tight as I dragged my lips across his a final time before squeezing and angling him back. Half-lidded eyes peered back at me, filled with blissed-out desire. "Get your cock out."

He shuddered.

I tugged him against me, trapping his cock, putting pressure against him. Steel pulsed behind his black jeans. The throb of his heartbeat was loud enough to reach my ears. I shifted one of my fingers, resting it over the life-giving vein on his neck.

"Let me take care of you."

Lips parting, Lucas closed his eyes, another shudder racking his perfect body.

"Show me your pretty cock and feed it to me." Nothing but rough gravel filled my tone, the need to possess him too damn tempting to ignore. "Matt." His eyes sprang open. "Cock out."

With fumbling hands that I suspected were as rare to him as a hot summer in Scotland, he unbuttoned and unzipped himself. I held still, refusing to break eye contact despite the desire to glance down and watch as he revealed himself.

After this, I wanted to shower him, feed him, wrap him in a blanket, and hold him close.

Have him be my backpack as we rode around the property, feeling the warm wind whipping around us.

The sounds of him releasing himself stopped, drawing my focus. I flexed my fingers once around his throat, and his lips parted further, his tongue darting out. I followed the movement, my gut clenching when I caught a flash of fang.

Fuck.

Only once had I felt fangs break my skin and someone take deep pulls. It had been a matter of necessity, a life-giving exercise rather than anything personal or even sexual. But the thought of Lucas drinking deeply…. A shudder trickled down my spine.

"Lift up," I instructed, releasing my hold on him. When he did, I tugged his jeans under his backside and finally took my fill.

I groaned, the sound tearing free unbidden, but rewarded with Lucas's gasp and the pearl of precum that escaped, I was more than okay with him knowing how turned on I was.

Long and with a thickness that would stretch my lips perfectly, his cock jutted out proudly. A thick vein ran the length. I salivated, eager to follow its journey, desperate to drop to his balls and suck each one into my mouth. Maybe when I did, I could press a finger deep inside him.

Would he come untouched? Would he come alive and let go, pant my name as he exploded?

Needing to find out what he felt like, I stroked his dick, trailing my finger up and down his velvet-soft skin. He held up his shirt without instruction, revealing his tight abs that clenched at my exploration.

"When was the last time someone took good care of you?" I shouldn't want to know. It had fuck all to do with me, but my curiosity refused to settle.

"Too long." A grunt followed when I dipped my fingers and caressed his balls.

"How long since someone swallowed you down and you released down their throat?"

His eyelashes fluttered, his chest shifting as he took in a lungful of air.

I smirked in satisfaction. "Do you want me to do that to you? Let you watch as I drink your cum?" My cock punched against my jeans, pissed the hell off that I was dragging this out.

He nodded, opening his eyes. "Yes."

When I raised my brows, a flash of frustration entered his gaze. My grin stretched wider. This here was the Lucas I was getting to know. Needy and desperate for a caretaker, yes—even if he didn't know it yet—but he was also a man who made it crystal fucking clear when I was pissing him off.

That alone was the cause of having a perpetual hard-on since meeting him.

"Yes, I want to watch as you drink my cum."

"Fucking perfect." I scooted back and dropped to my knees, never more grateful for my tall frame. I tugged Lucas right to the edge of the table and pulled his jeans down further so I could spread his thighs and get closer. Satisfied, I lifted my gaze and connected with his, making sure his eyes were on me as I took hold of his rock-hard cock and painted my lips with his precum.

A shuddery breath escaped him.

I quirked my lips, which earned me a narrowed gaze before I opened my mouth and sucked him down.

Immediately, his eyes rolled up, and he arched his back, thrust, and collapsed back on the table.

Satisfaction rolled through me, and a laugh would have escaped if I didn't have a mouthful and I weren't so ridiculously horny. I concentrated on his tells—his flexing muscles, his ragged breaths, his inability to stay still. As I sucked and licked, bobbed and caressed, I revelled in his scent, in his obvious need.

Fuck, he was glorious, a writhing mess of grunts and shifting hips, his back still arched as I held his butt tight to the edge of the table.

Pulling off with a pop, I grinned as he scrambled to reach me.

"Shh, I'm not going anywhere. I just need a taste of these," I said, running my tongue around his balls.

The dirty moan he released tightened my gut and drew my nuts high.

"With sounds like that, I'm going to come in my pants." I sucked one of his balls into my mouth, loving his ragged moan and liking even more when he lifted onto his elbows and peered down at me.

His eyes were wide, frenzied.

"Just tasting you, hearing you, is the biggest fucking turn-on." My voice was gravel, and I sucked his other ball into my mouth.

Lucas shuddered and parted his lips.

"You like that?" I prompted, running my finger over the end of his cock before gathering my spit and slicking it between his arse cheeks. "You like knowing how desperate you make me? Like the idea of me blowing a nut from sucking you off?"

"Fuck yes."

Warmth bloomed in my chest. Hearing Lucas swear was my second-favourite thing to come out of his mouth. His sexy moans and groans were obviously the first.

"In that case, do it. Fuck my mouth. Let's see how loud you can be, how deep you can go, and if you've got what it takes to make me explode."

I was all in, completely on board with him fucking my throat raw. The thought of coming untouched in my pants while swallowing his cum could quite possibly be my new obsession.

Fucking bring it.

And he did.

Putting his weight on his hands for full leverage,

he moved his hips like a piston, fucking my throat. I angled myself, lifting a little higher, relaxing my throat muscles.

Hard and fast, his cock dragged along my tongue, pushing fully until it was possible to swallow around him while he was wedged deep. As soon as I did, a dirty, needy moan burst out of him, along with desperate pleas of "Fuck… now… that's it… more," but it was Lucas gasping "Ethan" that was almost my undoing.

My dick throbbed, balls drawing high as a zing of pleasure zapped over my skin.

Any moment I was going to shoot my load. Fuck if a hum of pride didn't burst to life. He'd taken me at my word, fucking my mouth like it was his mission, seemingly determined to push himself over the edge and take me with him.

I slid my fingers between his cheeks, gathering spit on the way, my pad finding his tight opening. A single tap and he shuddered. A dip inside and Lucas lost momentum. A full finger slid in, a sweep across his prostate, and he froze, seated deep in my throat as jets of cum poured down my oesophagus.

Pulling back, wanting to drink him down, I dragged him along my tongue until I circled his glans.

That and the groaning of my name on repeat was all it took.

As his flavour exploded in my mouth, filling my senses, the desperate cry of "Ethan" as he chased his release, my cock twitched, my vision turning hazy as my orgasm barrelled through me.

I lapped as I came, determined to clean him completely even as my muscles clenched and my cum coated my jeans.

"Fuck." Lucas collapsed back against the table, his cock softening, fitting snugly in my mouth as I finished sucking and savouring the remnants of his release. "That was…." He trailed off, almost turning into a puddle against the rough-sawn table as his muscles relaxed completely.

I pulled off slowly, finishing with a tender kiss against his slit just as he peered down and made eye contact, watching the final attention I gave his dick. The gesture was tender as fuck, but hell, the man had earned it. He'd done exactly as I'd instructed.

I had copious amounts of sticky cum in my jeans to prove it.

Still on my knees, I pressed a kiss to his thigh. At the touch, he slowly blinked, his gaze clearing a little.

Screw that. I still had a plan, a list I wanted to get through. If I gave him the time to think about this,

Lucas the boss would reappear, right along with his shields.

That was the last thing I wanted.

Leaning back, I tugged off his jeans completely. "We're going to shower." His brows rose. "Together." I glanced at the hob that, thankfully, I'd turned off. "Then we're eating cold steak, and you can eat a damn carrot."

When his lips twitched, warmth swooped in my stomach. Earning a smile from him was as heady as running through Haldon Forest on the first day of spring in my quadruped form. The forest, with its towering trees and the fresh scent of pine and earth, was my sanctuary. Was I giving Lucas too much power? No doubt. It didn't matter that I was the one calling the shots, caring for him, and making sure he had what he needed. He definitely controlled every action and decision I made.

"Then we're going for that ride before taking a nap. After that, we're going to blow some shit up and finally take down an empire that deserves to be turned to dust."

I didn't ask for confirmation. Didn't need for him to give his approval. The way he sagged further into the table, giving himself over to the plan I laid out, told me everything I needed to know.

Mathew Lucas really was fucking dangerous, so fuck yes, I was going to dive in and give him what he needed. Consequences be damned.

CHAPTER 5

LUCAS

Having noodles for limbs wasn't conducive to being on my game. Officially, I wasn't. How could I possibly be with the way I'd all but begged Wilder to manhandle me? But with my thirst sated, my stomach full of steak and a bite of that damn carrot that he'd plonked on my plate, I couldn't regret anything.

It was impossible to have regrets when the chaos in my brain was quiet for the first time in—let's be real here—years.

A peace I'd not felt in decades offered me a bliss I didn't dare trust. And I shouldn't trust it. Putting my faith in a man just because he had the skill to make me shoot my load and quieten the mountain of voices laying out my responsibilities was likely the dumbest thing I could ever allow to happen.

Yet here I was, barely holding on to Wilder in a koala hug as we raced over red dirt. Freedom held us in a bubble of protection, sending a sweet breeze and the welcoming growl of the motorbike's engine.

A heated hand stroked my arm, squeezing lightly before letting go and returning to the throttle. The touch seared my skin, sending a pulse of heat to my stomach. Sure, my dick was interested, trapped against him. It was Wilder's cocky confidence, though, the speeds he took, the laughter when he turned swiftly, grabbing hold of me at the last second, as I wasn't joking about my noodle arms, that kept me smiling and my brain blissfully quiet.

With my cheek pressed against his heated back, I sighed, the sound so content, it sounded alien.

But still, I refused to overthink, to question. Maybe later, when reality came knocking, but for the moment, I found the energy to breathe Wilder in and wriggle my fingers against his stomach until I found the bare sliver of skin above the waistband of his clean jeans.

Warmth filled my cheeks. Wilder hadn't touched his dick—neither had I—yet him sucking me off and swallowing my cum had pushed him over the edge. Had I ever experienced anything so heady before? The truth was, the aftercare, the shower, the food, this right here—the combination melted not only my limbs but every single one of my hard-built defences.

I hoped to hell he didn't make me live to regret it.

At a tap on my hand, I lifted my head, angling a little as he glanced over his shoulder.

Those intense browns of his captured my attention, and it took me a moment to realise a small smile sat on his lips.

Soft smiles and gentle squeezes? How the hell had we reached this point?

I mentally shook my head and paid attention to his words.

"You ready to head back?"

We hadn't left the secure property border, not wanting to break free of the fences or interfere with the alert system setup. The situation in Canberra was too precarious for that. At least we had some good sense to rein in the desire to keep riding, continue heading west until we reached no-man's-land, where we could fall off the face of the earth for a while.

Reluctantly, I nodded. Thoughts of escaping meant I needed to get back to reality. To the responsibility never far away.

He studied my face a beat before he offered an up-nod and turned away.

I settled back into my position of cheek against

his back, pleased we'd decided to ride without helmets. I could enjoy this for a little longer. It wasn't like I hadn't chosen the life I led. Heck, for the most part, I loved it.

But sometimes…. I shrugged the thought away, grinning when Wilder revved the throttle and gunned it. I grasped on to the addictive joy, hollering a ridiculous "Whoop!" and for once not giving a damn about being embarrassed.

The revs increased, Wilder joining in by howling like a bloody wolf rather than the bear he was. A burst of deep, booming laughter followed, my own matching his as the cabin drew closer and closer.

Back to reality.

Slowing down, Wilder once again squeezed my forearm. "Nap first."

The argument froze on my tongue. We had so much to do, to prepare for.

"Just two hours, that's all," he added as he eased up on the throttle, edging closer to the cabin.

I loosened my muscles, having not realised just how tightly wound up I'd become when I thought about reality. Wilder had known, though. For a computer specialist, he had a talent for reading body language.

Or maybe it was just mine?

"Just two hours," I confirmed.

As he pulled to a stop, he angled to look at me, a pleased smile directed my way.

Despite my smirk, I rolled my eyes. "What?" I challenged with a fairly pathetic attempt at sass. I couldn't even fool myself that I wasn't loving the attention. "Two hours of sleep, and we'll have eight and a half hours before the meetings take place."

A buzz of discomfort worked its way into my system. Would that really be enough time? We still had—

"Off the bike."

Startled, I jumped off immediately.

"In the cabin, strip, and get your arse into bed."

I parted my lips, but at his arched brow, all fight left me. "How do you do that?"

"Because I'm right and you know it. You can't argue with common sense." He climbed off the bike and stood directly in front of me, close enough to touch, but he kept his hands to himself. "After two hours of sleep, you'll function better, work better, and be able to run the mission better. Correct?"

The arsehat was right, and from his smug grin, he knew it.

"You're also great at dishing out advice and orders, especially to your team about their wellbeing, but you take zero care of yourself."

Heat flushed my skin, embarrassment and indignation fluttering to the surface. "I take care of myself." My argument didn't hold a lick of conviction. If I didn't believe it, there was no way he did.

And how he even knew enough to call me out.... Bloody hell, was I actually surprised, considering how he'd behaved towards me, "handled" me? Because that's exactly what he'd been doing. I wasn't sure how to respond to that.

I should be annoyed. Incensed. Definitely calling him out and shutting him down.

"Matt."

The soft tone snapped my attention to his penetrating gaze.

"Let me do this for you."

I swallowed hard, loving and hating everything about the understanding evident in the depth of his brown eyes.

Could I afford to listen to him, let Wilder do this for me?

The hope—and plan—was to finally get Hornell in custody within a few hours. Wilder would then be on the next flight out of Australia. Life could then go back to normal. The thought left a bitter taste in my mouth, but it was what needed to happen.

Whisper soft, I agreed, "Okay." A few more hours, I could give him, allow myself stolen moments to shut out real life. And not a second more.

Wordlessly, Wilder nodded and placed his warm hand on my back, encouraging me to head inside. I followed his lead, one foot in front of the other, my muscles already relaxing, my thoughts settling.

"Let me check the systems and engage the security. I want you undressed and in bed, eyes closed and focussed on sleeping." Wilder punctuated his words with a kiss on my neck. A shudder zipped down my body, and goose bumps sprang to life.

"Fine." We stepped inside. Once in the doorway of the room, I paused and glanced at him.

He stood at the first security panel on this level, hand poised but eyes on me. "Okay?"

Was I?

I'd been tempted to ask him a million questions, starting with what on earth was happening here? But did I really want to know the answer?

I shook my head. *A few more hours.*

I spun away, thinking instead about following his directions. Concentrating on those alone allowed my mind to stop spinning.

Undress.

Get under the sheet.

Close my eyes.

Relax.

I totally had this.

And if, ten minutes later, his overheated body

pressed against my side and I just so happened to snuggle up to him, almost mirroring my koala hug from earlier, then so be it.

A few more hours to allow this to happen, to embrace the unexpected comfort. After that, all of this would be like it had never happened.

***

THE TRUSTED CONTACTS DURRANT HAD PULLED WERE divided into four areas: one in Canberra, another in Melbourne, one in Sydney, and the final one here in Queensland, just outside Brisbane's CBD.

The latter was where we'd ventured.

Confident we'd had no tail, we'd made it to the rendezvous point an hour ahead of schedule—after switching out the bike for an SUV. It allowed us to set up some equipment and prepare for our four arrivals.

Michaels and Shaw had travelled to Melbourne with Smythe and Hart providing tech support, while Chris and Kent took point back home in Sydney, with Callen in the country capital.

The setup in the old water station wasn't ideal, but it was off radar and suited the purpose to get us through the takedown.

"The access points are here." Wilder's deep

timbre, once as frustrating as a buzzing fly, had become a soothing caress.

I edged over in my rolling chair, stopping at his side to peer at his screen.

Less than five klicks away stood our target: a warehouse at the centre of the Queensland base of operations. While the location was based on the intel Durrant had managed to get from Jefferson, who'd been quick to share his involvement once he'd been brought in and Callen had revealed the extent of our intel, we were confident with the validity.

Deep dives, satellite footage, and some impressive hacking from Hart had consolidated the evidence we needed to forge ahead. But this whole mission remained precarious.

Sure, we were working under Durrant's orders, like we always were, but considering the scope and a small section of the Defence Ministry's involvement, we really were entering the viper's den—specifically, four of them.

"And the old gas tunnels are completely cut off?" I asked.

It was something Wilder had discovered when studying the blueprints. In theory, the tunnels could be used as an escape route—for those who were able to shift into smaller forms.

"Definitely," he confirmed. "We can ensure all

access points are covered, but the tunnels are no longer accessible."

I bobbed my head. "I've spoken to Callen. Murdock's provided the last known location of Hornell." It stung that we wouldn't be there, but it seemed poetic almost that Michaels and Shaw would be the ones to take him down in Melbourne. Bearing in mind all they'd been through over a year back when Hornell first jumped onto our radar, I knew they'd pull out all the stops to make it happen.

We all would.

"Have you had any success with discovering potential fail-safes?" I asked. It was a point Hart had raised. A man like Hornell would not come in quietly. Not only were his resources extensive—and I was sure we didn't know the half of it—but he had a lot to lose.

The thirst for his blood made me twitch. Not that I'd drink a drop of the toxic crap I was sure ran through his poisoned veins. But watch his blood stain the ground? I wouldn't miss a wink of sleep if that was how it went down.

"Not yet."

I glanced at Wilder, taking in his expression. It matched his pissed-off voice.

"I'm still searching. I also have a couple of trusted

contacts back home who're offering support." He made eye contact, then lifted his brow, no doubt reading my reaction. "I trust them."

We maintained contact for a couple of beats before I nodded. Sure, my skin itched at the unknown, and I was struggling over not having all the answers and relying on people I hadn't personally vetted, but this was one of those times I had to trust my gut.

I settled on "Okay."

He bobbed his head, a pleased smile tugging at the corners of his lips.

"I'm going to suit up. We should have company in a few minutes."

As I turned, I ignored his frown. Wilder had no say in the execution of this operation. While I appreciated all he was doing and the contacts he'd reached out to for additional support, Durrant had tasked me with the running of the mission.

I'd disseminated the information and the schedule to each member of my unit, including Callen and Durrant despite their higher ranking. They trusted me to make this run like clockwork. Four operations, all carried out simultaneously, in three states and one territory.

That I had to suit up in my fatigues and arm

myself, ready to be called in for backup, wasn't ideal, but Wilder out there wouldn't fly. Not only was he here without the proper papers, but if shit hit the fan, he needed to be far away from this.

Plus, he could handle all the comms and the tech as well as I could. Add in the fact that he'd admitted he hadn't been boots on the ground in almost twenty years—unlike me—there was no other alternative but for him to take point if I needed to offer additional tactical support.

As I pulled on the SICB-supplied tactical vest, the door opened to the room we'd allocated as our hub of operations. The light from the open doorway disappeared almost immediately, blocked out, I expected, by a prickly bear. A quick glance revealed Wilder. His large frame filled the doorway. At the sight of him, his tight jaw and intense gaze, my gut clenched.

That he didn't like the idea of me being in the thick of gunfire or exposed to claws and teeth didn't help the uncomfortable swirl in my stomach. There was nothing permanent with what was happening between us. We hadn't discussed it, but we didn't need to.

The heat between us was fast and thrilling and would burn out to cinders in a matter of hours.

So why did my slow-beating heart pick up when I took him in and imagined this all being over?

"Promise me something."

My brows shot high, not expecting those words. "What's that?"

"That if you have to provide backup, you'll return unharmed."

Once again my pulse sped up even as I shook my head while my eyes roamed his expression. "I can't promise that."

Wilder clenched his jaw, and he took a large stride into the small room, bringing himself directly before me so I had to tilt my head to meet his gaze. "Promise you'll *try*." From the scrunch of his nose, it seemed that word was distasteful. "Yes, you have a mission. Yes, you have a team you'll be supporting. But you also need to put yourself first."

"What?" Confusion had me backing up a step. "I'm team leader. My job is to protect my unit and make sure the job is done. I pledged my allegiance to my country, my agency, my team. I'll do whatever it takes to make that happen."

More than that, my daughter would be out there. She would always come first.

"For fuck's sake." A sneer followed. "This is what's wrong with all fucking government agencies. Do I need to remind you that *your* government, *your* defence forces are the reason you're here right now, putting your life on the line? Fuck, Matt, *your* fucking government has a warrant to bring you in. You're telling me they're the ones you're willing to die for if necessary?" Wilder shook his head in disgust, anger making his body shake.

Taken aback by his outburst, it took me a moment to gather my thoughts enough to react. "You don't have to be here. I'm grateful that you are, and you being here is helpful." Tightening my fists, I held back the rising tide of anger. "But don't you dare question my loyalty or the reasons why I do this. My team is counting on me. This mission is bigger than us."

Wilder's eyes flashed with a mix of frustration and desperation. "I'm not questioning your abilities, Matt. I know you're good at what you do. But I see you throwing yourself into this like you're trying to prove something to someone who doesn't give a shit about you."

I stepped closer, refusing to back down. "It's not about proving anything, Ethan. It's about doing what's right. It's about stopping Hornell and saving lives. You think I don't know the risks? Every time I suit up, I know it might be my last mission. But if not me, then who?"

His jaw clenched again, and he gripped the edge

of the table to our right so hard, I thought it might snap. "And if you go down? What happens to your team then? Have you thought about that? You're so damn focussed on the mission that you're ignoring the most important part—keeping yourself alive so you can lead them."

I took a deep breath, trying to steady my nerves. "I lead by example. If they see me hesitating, second-guessing, then they will too. I need them to trust that I'll make the right calls, that I'll be there when they need me." Even more so because those arriving in just a few moments weren't my usual crew, despite me knowing three of the four individuals. They were stepping into this with no history with my unit. Their sole motivation was their loyalty and allegiance to Durrant.

That was enough for me.

Wilder's expression softened but only slightly. "I get that. I do. But you're more than just a leader. You're… You're important to people. To me. And it scares the hell out of me to think that you might not come back."

The admission caught me off guard. For a moment, the walls I'd built around myself wavered. "Wilder, I appreciate that you care. But right now, I need you to trust me. Trust that I know what I'm doing and that I'm prepared for whatever comes our way."

He nodded, but the tension didn't leave his body. "I trust you, Matt. It's the situation I don't trust. Just... promise me you'll do everything you can to come back. Not for the government, not for the agency. For the people who care about you. For me."

For him?

But that wasn't what this was meant to be.

Did I want more? Could I trust him enough to accept the possibility?

I looked him in the eye, seeing the fear and concern that he tried so hard to hide. "I'll do my best, Ethan. But I can't make any guarantees. All I can promise is that I'll fight like hell to see this through."

He took a step back, exhaling slowly. "That's all I can ask for, I guess. Just... be careful out there."

He made it sound like a done deal—me needing to go in as backup. My gut twisted, telling me I thought he was right.

We hadn't had enough time to prepare. We didn't fully know what we were walking into.

With a nod, I turned towards the door, feeling the weight of his words and the impending mission pressing down on me. "We will be. Now let's get ready. Our team is counting on us."

With my heart thumping unsteadily, I headed to

the main hub, which was more of a glorified makeshift computer lab than I was used to. We'd make it work, though.

Despite everything being murky between us, Wilder's—Ethan's—concern shouldn't have been as unexpected as it was. In truth, his determination, him following me and sharing his thoughts, spun me out. What they also did, though, was quieten the brewing anxiety of seeing my daughter again.

At least for a few minutes.

Now, nerves played havoc with my emotions. Since Ethan had made the call, I didn't know if she was aware of my presence. While I hadn't asked Wilder to withhold information about me being in Brisbane, I hadn't asked him if he'd told her or not.

Right or wrong, though, two vehicles approached, so I was about to find out exactly what Valeria knew.

Taking control of myself, I regulated my heartbeat and ensured my breaths returned to the usual slow inhale and exhale. "Are you ready?" Authority clung to my question.

"Yup." He held my gaze for a beat before offering an up-nod and focussing back on the security feed.

I took to the mic that would connect me to the three other teams. "Alpha Strike, Bravo Force, Charlie Squad, this is Delta Recon. Are you reading? Over."

Callen answered first. "Alpha Strike checking in. Over."

"Bravo Force checking in. Over," Kent responded.

Smythe responded last. "Charlie Squad checking in. Over."

"Our additions are thirty seconds out. Please confirm your arrivals." We'd provided each of Durrant's contacts with an overview, but due to the nature of the op, some elements were too risky to share in any manner other than face to face.

All three teams responded with similar times. There was something to be said about agents and professionals and their ability to keep on schedule. It seriously helped my stress levels.

"Vehicles are pulling up now," Wilder said.

I nodded. "Got it." I returned to my mic, reaching out to our teams. "0900 exactly, Brisbane time, all teams are to move in. They're to be in position by 0855. Copy?"

We'd already been over everything required, the locations, what each objective was. Our focus here in Brisbane, at the warehouse a few short klicks away, was a central server that linked all Hornell's networks nationally and overseas.

When all three units confirmed, we silenced communication, and I turned to the door where

Wilder had given access to the four new additions to our unit.

Alinta entered first, her scowling face softening immediately when she spotted me. "Lucas. It's been a long time, old friend."

I stepped closer and greeted her with a handshake and a hug. As a vampire almost twice my age, Alinta had experience and impressive skills. I had nothing but respect for her. I also knew she was stepping out of her sabbatical as a favour to Durrant.

"It's good to see you, Alinta. It's been too long."

She squeezed my arm, and I suspected she was thinking back to the last time we saw each other—Maya's twilight vigil. My heart tightened at the memory, at the betrayal. I shook it away, not wanting any thought of my daughter's mother to touch me… or Valeria.

It was no mistake that I'd wanted Alinta with the Brisbane unit alongside Valeria. It was difficult enough not to be joining them in the first wave by instead running the op from here. But at least with Alinta, a seasoned agent—one of many hats she'd worn over her years—my daughter would be well protected.

She also knew the truth, one of the very few individuals who did.

Alinta thinned her lips, clamping them together

as movement at the door caught our focus. That reaction alone told me Valeria was here and pissed. Sympathy sparked in Alinta's gaze before she stepped away, leaving me a direct view of Valeria.

She was beautiful and so, so mad. Fire lit her eyes, looking so much like her mother's, my heart squeezed.

"Valeria," I said softly. The need to reach out and hold her tight made it difficult to stay put. For as much as my daughter didn't think I knew her, I could read her well enough. Everything about her tall frame—just an inch shy of my own—and her scowl that flickered to indifference as I watched told me to back off.

Hurt lacerated my chest, and as much as she may have thought I deserved it, I could never regret it all. Her being alive before me with the ability to bleed defiance was fundamentally the reason why I made the decisions I had. And that she wanted nothing to do with me? It was a burden I'd continue to bear as long as she lived and breathed.

Valeria looked away first, stalking to the table and taking a seat. I tracked her movements before glancing away, my gaze meeting Wilder's briefly. Unable to handle his curiosity or his sympathy, I focussed on the last two members.

Dharrun, a wolf shifter from Perth who I didn't

know personally. What I did know was that he was an Indigenous elder as well as a lieutenant in the WA Enforcement Unit. That Durrant trusted him meant I would too.

I reached out and shook his hand. "Thanks for coming, Lieutenant."

"Agent Lucas," he greeted. "Not quite the call I expected to be receiving yesterday, but if the SICB's director needs me, I'm here."

"We all appreciate that."

He stepped aside and headed to the table, leaving me to welcome Tarka.

The bear was all smiles and beefy limbs as he wrapped me up in a giant hug. Perhaps not the most professional of greetings, but we'd known each other for decades—ever since we'd both joined the SICB. He'd since flown the coop, now owning his own security firm, but his name on Durrant's list made complete sense.

"Good to see you, Mattie." The behemoth of a man lifted me off my feet, causing heat to sting my cheeks and warm familiarity to roll in my gut. "You're a sight for sore eyes." He stepped back, his meaty hand on my shoulder. "You've got some real shit going on here that needs some specialist atten-tion, huh?" He winked and glanced around the room, pausing on Wilder.

I followed his gaze, taking in Wilder's expression. With his jaw clenched, he didn't look pleased.

Tarka's huff of amusement dragged my attention back to him. "Looks like you're keeping interesting company these days."

"Behave," I admonished with exactly zero heat. Tarka was almost impossible to keep in line. It was his desire to not follow orders rather than his inability that had him leave the SICB and start his own firm. Honestly, we'd been through so much together over the years. His being here, stepping back into the fold for me—as I was sure Durrant added him because she knew he wouldn't refuse a request from me—meant something. "Thanks for coming."

"With you and Durrant at the helm and the glorious Alinta here, no way would I miss it." He stepped to my side, and we glanced at the table. "And our beautiful Vally. How are you doing, kiddo?"

Valeria rolled her eyes. "Don't start, T. Get your arse over here so we can get the final details of this mission and I can get the fuck outta here." She glanced away, refusing to even make eye contact.

"Holy shit," Tarka whispered, though everyone in the room could hear. "It just dropped twenty degrees in here, right? Talk about ice burn."

Alinta's huffed "Tarka" had him smirking. He shot me a wink before he headed over to the large table. Envy tightened my chest when he sat heavily next to Valeria and tugged her to his side. When he dotted a kiss on her head and she didn't push him away, I looked away quickly, the dull ache rapidly growing to the size of a boulder.

This was a mistake, having her come to Brisbane.

The hell was I thinking?

I should have refused, told Durrant not to get her involved.

If she got hurt just because I wanted to see her, how on earth could I live with myself?

Thoughts layered in my brain—the what-ifs and could-have-beens piling higher and higher, growing, becoming heavy.

Warmth at my side registered at the edges of my mind, the soft "Hey" penetrating.

Shit.

Wilder.

He stood close, blocking my view of the table.

Making eye contact, we stared at each other in silence, just for a beat, but long enough to help me take control of my thoughts. A nod later, he stepped away, leaving his piercing heat clinging to my side.

I focussed on the feeling, the warmth he offered, not just in his touch but the gentle intervention. How the man just knew I was spiralling should have terrified me completely. Instead, it bolstered me and reminded me of who I was and what was at stake.

No more distractions. No more feeling sorry for myself, wishing for things that may never happen.

"Let's get right to it," I started, joining the group at the table, Wilder at my side and even my daughter glancing my way, a new curiosity in her gaze.

CHAPTER 6
WILDER

"Head out in five."

The group around the table nodded at Matt's instruction—since I'd swallowed him down, I struggled to think of him as Agent Lucas anymore—and stood, getting on with whatever they intended in the five minutes before they jumped back into the two vehicles they'd arrived in.

Amusement jabbed at my chest at the surreal moment. There was fuck all funny about the situation, but the very fact that I was working with past and present government agents gave me cause to pause. Add in that this wasn't officially sanctioned, and hell yes, I was entertained.

It was only Matt's stiff shoulders and take-no-nonsense expression that stopped me smirking. His life had been nonstop for almost a week, though I suspected that wasn't anything super different. Instead, it was the warrant, him watching his carefully constructed and controlled world not only showing signs of cracking but full-on crumbling around him.

Then there was the animosity from his daughter.

Finding it difficult to not openly stare at Valeria, I forced my attention to Matt. While it wasn't exactly difficult to look at him, to do so without the ghost of his touch, his taste teasing me was another story.

He'd already explained the situation in finer detail to the crew of four, then the rest of the teams joined in after fifteen minutes of the briefing. New intel indicated Murdock had involved a smaller sector of the Defence Ministry than previously expected. The relief had been palpable around the table. For me, not so much, as I couldn't give a flying fuck.

This wasn't my government, and since my expectation of the Aussie government was no better than the shitshow I'd experienced back home in the UK, I had zero investment in if they weren't as corrupt as we suspected or not.

I cast a glance at Matt. He cared. Poor arsehole.

I remembered when I had such an allegiance, but all that had gotten me was an identity wipe and the years I'd dedicated to protecting my country smashed to smithereens.

Officially, I'd never worked for the UK's cyber unit. While I'd quit, walking away after refusing to follow a direct order, it had stung for a while there. Deleting my very existence was a shithead move by the unit's head honcho.

I may have celebrated extra hard when, two years later, I watched on livestream the moment he was arrested for a whole bunch of corruption charges, which I may or may not have had a hand in digging up and dumping on the police's doorstep.

So reluctantly, I understood Matt's frustration, his determination to chop off the heads of the multiple vipers that had too much power in this country. For his sake, I hoped his government didn't turn its back on him.

I wasn't sure how he'd handle that.

"You ready?"

My gaze snapped to Matt's, his question catching me off guard. I'd been staring at him, focussing on the way he tried not to watch Valeria.

"Yeah. Just checking the comms now," I answered swiftly, turning my attention to the screen. I readjusted my headset and worked through the system checks that would give me access to all four comms, plus Matt's, and the additional three in the different locations around the country as well.

The screen before me displayed information on each team in the different states, giving me visual alerts that matched the comms. That way there'd be no confusion about who I was speaking to or what was happening.

With the joint operation and the timing being paramount, fuck-ups would be easy. No way would I let that happen if I could help it.

Was I too invested? Discomfort shifted in my chest at f my possible answer. It was best I avoided thinking about it.

Instead, I opened the comms to Hart. Thank fuck he was on the other end. Someone I could rely on. Admittedly, how we'd left things had been a little strained, but one, fuck him for thinking I was in league with the master plan or some shit. And hello, the guy had lost his sense of humour since being all loved-up.

I knew my involvement. Took responsibility for it. It was the only reason I was here.

I refused to inhale deeply to absorb Lucas's addictive scent.

He could not be the reason I was still here and so invested.

"Hart," I said through a private line.

"Wilder."

He didn't sound as pissed, so that was something. I didn't have many people I could call friends left in the world. Honestly, I wasn't sure Hart was even on that short list, but he was close to making it, despite the tiger taking a swing at me.

"How's Smythe doing?"

There was an uncomfortable pause. It seeped into my bones. It felt weird, being all polite and caring and shit.

"He's good," Hart finally answered. Wariness clung to his tone. I'd put that there, was absolutely responsible for it.

I sighed. "That's good, man. I'm pleased for you."

A huff of laughter travelled to my earpiece. "You are, huh?"

"The fact that he's stopping you from being so much of a moody prick means Smythe's probably good for you." My lips twitched, and I became aware of Matt sitting at my side, his face angled my way. I cleared my throat.

"I'd say it takes one to know one, but you know, you're a moodier cunt than me, so...," he dragged out with a short-lived laugh.

Another smile twitched my lips, my shoulders

easing. Being back on familiar ground with Hart was a relief.

"You've got this, yeah?"

I bit back my sigh at his serious question, hating the switch in tone. Not that I didn't understand why he felt the need. "You know I do."

"All right, then. In that case, let's get this shit-show on the road. Keep your line open."

No shit, Sherlock. I rolled my eyes. Rather than calling him out, I responded, "Over and out."

The sound of the codes being entered to open the secure door drifted through the room. I looked that way and to see our four team members about to head out. I offered them a nod as they left, aware of Matt at my side staring in the same direction.

Valeria looked once at her dad before her gaze landed on me. I arched my brow in challenge or in question—I wasn't sure yet. I hadn't spoken to her beyond answering a couple of her questions during the briefing. Her being pissed at her dad, though, didn't sit right. While he said he deserved it—and likely he did—Matt was a good guy and clearly loved his daughter. That he was hurting twisted my gut more than it should.

Without a word, she spun on her heel and closed the door behind her.

Families could be screwed-up units. Experience and heartache had taught me that over the years.

Not glancing Matt's way, I spoke quietly, unable to stop myself. "She'll be okay."

I felt his eyes on me, but I refused to look. Matt was a distraction I couldn't afford, especially when his daughter's life was involved. I was under no illusion about how fucking wrong this mission could go.

Determination pulsed through me. We needed to get this bullshit over.

"Ready?" I asked Matt, studying the live satellite feed I'd hacked into. There was no movement at the location where our unit was heading.

"Ready." I clocked his short nod and tracked our unit's journey.

"Three minutes out," I said into comms.

The trackers in their earpieces moved on the screen, edging closer to their park point. Right on schedule, the dots stopped before moving more slowly, the group of four now on foot. "They're on target. Two minutes from the wait point," I said to Lucas. My job was to keep a close eye on the unit while focussing on the satellite images of the area.

Matt liaised with the other units and listened out for chatter.

Tension pulsed against me, Matt's colliding with my own.

I confirmed, "One minute," keeping a steady eye on the images and listening to the soft breaths coming from Dharrun and Tarka. Unsurprisingly, the two vampires remained silent—not a whisper of breaths coming from them.

"On location."

Matt repeated the information to the three unit leaders, and we waited, watching the clock as I double-checked the satellite imagery, still pissed we couldn't get eyes inside the building. I hated being impressed that we couldn't get visual access. Whoever had set up the facility but had not included cameras was smart.

Hell, we couldn't even access a single camera on the employees' mobile phones. After finding an old order for a dead-zone safe to be delivered to the premises, it made sense that all phones and electrical devices brought into the facility were stowed away.

It was also the reason why we didn't give our team cameras. We suspected there'd be some sort of tracking system that alerted their security to video signals.

"One minute." Adrenaline swept up my spine. It had been a long time since I'd worked on any mission and supported agents on the ground. An uptick of my pulse reminded me what a rush it could be.

"In position and on countdown," Matt said through the comms.

"Copy that," Alinta answered, taking point.

I held my breath, watching the clock, aware all four units would be set to go in thirty seconds. This needed to work.

"Approaching the door," Alinta whispered into the comms.

"Copy that," I replied, watching their progress on the satellite feed from my position in the command centre. The exterior of the warehouse was clear, but the real danger lay within. A server room sounded like it wouldn't be an issue, but it was heavily guarded.

Alinta knelt at the door, swiftly working on the lock. Her nimble fingers danced over the keypad, bypassing the security system with practiced ease. The door clicked open, and the team slipped inside.

All visuals were lost, the satellite imagery no longer of use.

"Stay sharp," Alinta murmured, her voice barely audible.

They advanced quietly, their synchronised move-ments reflected by the trackers pulsing on my screen. The sound of footsteps echoed in the distance, drifting through their comms, and the team froze. I stilled, tense, waiting for a sign.

"Take them out," Alinta commanded.

The team sprang into action. Shots were fired. Two heavy drops followed. Valeria moved with speed, her position jumping. A grunt, a thud. The fight was over in seconds.

"Clear," Dharrun reported, his voice calm.

Two more "Clears" followed before Alinta spoke. "Movement ahead."

I watched on, listening carefully, relieved to hear a soft thud and Tarka's deep "Clear."

"Good work," Matt said through the comms. "Move to the server room."

They continued their advance, encountering minimal resistance. Each skirmish was dealt with swiftly and efficiently, the team's experience evident in every move. Durrant's request for their assistance became clearer and clearer.

"The server's ahead," Alinta reported.

"There should be a heavily fortified door." Matt's fingers flew over the keyboard, the blueprints appearing on the screen.

"Tarka, you're up," Alinta instructed.

While Tarka set up the small explosives, I studied the satellite imagery, looking for anomalies and changes. The detonation would be small and contained. It shouldn't draw any interest from outside forces.

"Fire in the hole," Tarka said. I watched their trackers move away from the server area.

A small bang, loud enough to alert everyone in the facility, echoed through the comms.

"Move, move, move," Alinta shouted.

Two pops of tranq guns, thuds, and the alarm that had pierced the air cut out.

"Downloading now," Valeria said. "Cover me."

Valeria was responsible for downloading the information on the servers before Dharrun stepped in to upload shutdown protocols. The minutes dragged on, tension thick in the air, not made any better by the strain tightening Matt's frame.

"Come on, come on," I muttered to myself, watching the progress bar on my screen.

Then, through the satellite feed, I saw the incoming vehicles. My heart skipped a beat.

"Incoming vehicles," I said into the comms. "Three SUVs, heavily armed. ETA four minutes."

"Damn it," Valeria hissed. "We need more time."

"They won't reach you."

Eyes wide, my head swivelled as Matt shot out of his chair.

Gaze on me and jaw tight, he nodded as he took hold of his comms pack and latched it onto his belt. "I'm intercepting."

Fear sliced through me.

"Finish the upload and get out," he said into the comms, but his eyes remained on me, unwavering.

"Roger that," Valeria replied.

And Matt was moving with no time to spare.

Fuck, fuck, fuck.

I watched the incoming vehicles, checking their progress. Lucas needed to hurry, and I fucking hated it. As he angled towards the door just as it beeped open, his gaze snagged mine.

Stay safe, I silently pleaded, thinking not for the first time that life would have been so much easier if I hadn't jumped on that damn plane. "Don't fucking die," I growled.

A slight uptick of a barely there smile and the arsehole was gone.

I took a breath, saying, "Three minutes out," and double-checked I was hooked into the comms of the other three units now that Matt was racing towards the three vehicles.

He'd be fine. Of course he would. He had to be. Hell, the vampire had been doing this job long before I was born. I put those words on repeat in my head, my new mantra. I needed to focus.

Inside the warehouse, the team finished the upload. The red upload turned to green on my screen.

"We're done," Alinta said. "Moving out."

The team moved quickly, retracing their steps through the warehouse. But as they neared the exit, a pop of gunfire sounded.

Fuck, I hated this. Being blind to their movements. Not seeing what was coming their way shot a bolt of frustration through my veins.

"Contact!" Valeria shouted, opening fire.

The fight sounded intense. Bullets flew, the sound deafening through the comms. Valeria and Alinta provided covering fire while Dharrun and Tarka engaged the guards in close combat, judging by the grunts and shouts between them.

"I see the SUVs." Matt's voice held steel I'd not heard before.

"Movement in the front seat of the left," I said quickly, zooming in as much as possible on the unfolding scene. The sound of gunfire echoed through the comms as Matt engaged the SUVs. One vehicle spun out, the back tyre bursting, the side smashing into a concrete building. Rather than continuing to the warehouse, the middle SUV stopped, opening fire.

Slamming on the brake, Matt turned, ramming the black Jeep. The crunch and grind of metal filled my ears, as did Matt's grunt.

"Fuckers."

"Driver's side," I instructed quickly, not having time to laugh at how pissed off Matt was.

Just as the driver edged out, gun aimed, he fell to the ground.

Holy shit.

Matt was a dead shot, which shouldn't have been a surprise.

I held my breath, gaze drifting between the placement of our unit and the satellite footage on Matt. My brows shot high as Matt took down a man mid-transformation. He fought with a ferocity I had rarely seen, taking out a second person with what I was sure was one punch and then a snap of his neck.

He moved with lethal grace, his speed and strength unmatched.

"Guards down," Alinta said. "Move out."

Outside, Matt continued to battle the incoming SUVs. He took out the second vehicle, preventing it from continuing its journey with a burst of gunfire, but the third one managed to get past him. The reinforcements were closing in on the warehouse.

"Lucas, the third SUV!" I urged, watching the satellite feed anxiously.

"Shit," he grunted, taking cover behind his vehicle. "I need to buy them more time."

He was within view of the warehouse, the SUV barely five seconds out.

Inside, the team finally reached the exit. They burst out into the daylight, running towards their vehicles, but their path was blocked by the remaining SUV, which braked sharply before the exit.

"Down!" Valeria shouted, diving for cover as the incoming guards spilled out of the Jeep and opened fire.

The team returned shots, pops and bangs exploding in a cacophony. Dharrun took out a guard with a well-placed shot, while Alinta provided suppressing fire. Dharrun and Tarka engaged the force in—

The power went out, plunging me into darkness. I cursed, fumbling for the switch to the backup generator.

Before I could get it running, an explosion rocked the building. My heart stopped as I heard footsteps, heavy and purposeful, approaching.

My fingers flexed, seeking out the knife I kept on my belt. I didn't expect that would do any good with the firepower I suspected was breaching the door.

"Lucas, come in?"

Not even static came down the line.

"Fuck," I shouted. There was only one way to handle this. "Bring it," I growled, shifting into my grizzly bear form. The transformation was quick, painless, and the effects immediate.

My hearing sharpened as power pulsed through my limbs.

Relying on my senses, I charged the intruders as they breached the now-unlocked door, my massive form wreaking havoc. Equipment shattered around me as I maimed and scratched and bit, groping for every piece of flesh I could sink my teeth into.

Gratified that two bodies now lay at my feet, I growled deep and low as the sound outside the room stopped close to the door. More were coming and about to infiltrate.

A sharp pain exploded in my side, and I roared in fury, swiping at my attackers. I spun, anger trailing a hot path through my veins that two mercenaries had managed to get behind me. I struck out but wobbled, missing the female tiger staring impassively at me. I could feel my strength waning, but I fought on with a burst of power, lunging at the wolf in human form at her side, determination fuelling me.

Before I latched on, a heavy blow to my head sent me sprawling. I fell with a grunt, pain hot and thick in both my head and my side. I felt a prick in my neck. Darkness closed in, and the last thing I heard was a voice saying, "Yeah, we've got him. We'll be in the air in twenty."

Fear for Matt, for our mission, for everything we had fought for consumed me as I slipped into unconsciousness.

Voices penetrated my brain, drawing me back to consciousness. They were muffled behind a closed door. Keeping my eyes shut, I listened carefully, trying to get my bearings before attempting to open my eyelids.

A dripping tap. A radio playing. A scratch of a heavy boot on concrete.

The floor beneath me was cold, also concrete. Dampness infiltrated the walls, having set into the plaster. Nothing but darkness behind my closed eyelids. No sliver of light. No windows?

A dull thud. Just one. *Duh-dum.*

A single heartbeat.

I waited, but no more came.

A vampire for sure. No other creature's heart beat like that. That I could hear it now meant they were excited, scared, or fucking furious.

I took stock.

My limbs ached, more from being flat on the cold floor than from injury. Dried blood was crusted on the side of my face, no doubt matting my hair and my beard. That would be a shit to get out.

My clothes were almost non-existent. Remembering that I'd shifted, wrecking my clothes in the process, I was surprised I now wore sweatpants. They were ill-fitting and tight. I sniffed, finding only my blood and sweat and minimal traces of Matt's earthy smell still on my skin. Matt. The hell had happened? Was he okay? The unit?

Fuck.

No longer able to resist, I opened my eyes. My sight readjusted quickly, and I zeroed in on the metal door before taking in the bare room, the only light spilling from the single flush-with-the-ceiling fixture above. It was dull—deliberately so, I suspected.

Duh-dum.

I froze before sitting upright and spinning to peer behind me.

Valeria.

My eyes sprang wide, my heart jumping up a notch as I took in her still form. Like me, her wrists were bound with the metal cuffs I recognised as being approved by government agencies. There'd be no breaking free from them.

Her shirt was torn, and dried blood was spread along her cheek and down her right arm.

What the hell was she doing here?

Questions raced through my brain. The last time I'd seen the unit, it was under fire. But there was just one vehicle. The team had appeared to have the upper hand.

Matt had been left with two people to take out. Sure, I'd been worried, but not for a second did I think he couldn't handle himself. Nor the team their mission.

"Valeria," I whispered before stilling. The voice outside cut off. *Fuck it.* I raised my voice. "Valeria." Assuming they were supes outside, they already knew I was awake.

I shifted my leg, a clank of metal drawing my attention.

The bastard pieces of shit.

A chain was fastened around my right ankle, which locked to a metal loop into the concrete. I barely kept my growl at bay. I needed to wake Valeria up and figure out what went wrong.

I inhaled again, deeper. The tinge of smoke stung my nose. I squinted, gaze roaming over Valeria once more. The fabric of her shirt was singed, a black smudge on her left arm and her forehead.

None of that was caused by gunfire.

Something had burned quite severely for it to have penetrated her tactical clothes like this.

I tried again. "Valeria, you need to wake up." I

ignored the scuff of a boot. It was a few metres away and wasn't accompanied by footsteps. For whatever reason, whoever was outside wasn't storming in just yet despite knowing I was awake.

"Valeria, wake the fuck up." I reached out, stretching, and finally found purchase on her booted foot. I took hold and shook none too gently. "Valeria."

A groan and her fingers twitched.

Thank fuck.

"That's it. Rise and shine, Vally. Time to get your head back in the game."

A grunt this time and her shoulders moved, her hand rising at the same time to strike an invisible assailant.

"Valeria." My tone brooked no nonsense, and her wild eyes finally landed on me.

A beat and another, and then her panic eased, recognition entering her gaze. "Wilder?"

"Yup. Hey, roomie." My mouth stretched wide, cracking the blood on the side of my face. "Nap time's over."

She blinked once before shaking her head and wincing.

"What's wrong?"

I'd been hit and maybe stabbed, and I thought drugged, but I was fully healed. It meant we'd been here for at least four hours. As a vampire, she healed a lot faster than I did.

"I think I was drugged." She pushed the heel of her hand against her temple. "My head's fuzzy."

My brows shot high. Either they had some pretty powerful drug that could knock a vamp on their arse for hours or they'd been giving her a top-up.

"Other than that, any injuries?"

"No. I took a bullet, but it was in and out." She rotated her right arm. "All healed." She looked me up and down. "What happened to you?"

I clenched my jaw but didn't answer, pissed off at the very thought of being put on my arse.

"The base was a wreck."

Surprise jolted me upright. "You all made it back to the base?" Did that mean Matt had too? Was he okay?

Her expression shuttered, her emotion unreadable, putting me on high alert.

"I arrived at the base first. We were split from the attack coming from the SUV. Alinta instructed me to take the vehicle closest to me."

The burning need to ask about her dad raised the hair on the back of my neck, but I kept quiet as I saw her processing everything that happened. A crease appeared between her brows, the gesture so like Matt's that unfamiliar emotion lodged in my throat.

"I went straight to the base and saw the unit on fire. I came in after you, unsure what had happened." Questions filled her gaze.

"The compound was compromised. I took two down that I'm sure of. I didn't know the northern entrance had been infiltrated until it was too late," I admitted, not holding back my growl of frustration. "That was immediately after you all exited the facility and went under fire."

That I didn't see a team coming for me grated. How the fuck had I not seen them?

"I saw the room was trashed. You weren't there, but I heard an engine out the back. They completely took me by surprise." Her frustration was palpable. Relatable.

The need to know pushed me to finally ask, "The rest of the team?" *Your dad?*

"All were okay when I left."

I narrowed my gaze, needing more.

She huffed out a breath, and I could just imagine what she would have been like as a teenager pissed off with her dad. Which was all levels of ridiculous. Sure, she may only have looked to be in her mid-twenties, but I knew she was at least a few years older than me.

"My father had his fangs to someone's throat as I drove past. He was holding his own."

That was good. My shoulders relaxed.

"So, you and Daddy dearest, huh?"

And they tensed right back up.

"I think the more pressing matter is where the fuck we are and why we're even here."

A one-shoulder shrug was her reply as she stared at me with open curiosity.

"You don't seem super concerned about the situation we're in." I narrowed my gaze at her.

With her shoulders relaxed and her expression appearing like she didn't give a shit, Valeria could just as well have been hanging around to buy a cinema ticket rather than sitting on a cold floor with a foggy head, locked up.

"Not the first time I've been in this kind of situation." Her lips quirked, and fuck it all to hell, a huff of amusement escaped me. She shuffled until her back pressed against the wall. "Plus it gives us the chance to catch up. I don't want all the deets, 'cause gross, but you and the old man, what's up with that?"

The hell was happening here?

I glanced around the room again, looking for an exit that may have magically appeared. Disappointed that none had, I considered calling out to our captors. Figuring out what was going on—hell, having my nipples clamped and volts shot to them—was absolutely preferable to getting the third degree from Matt's daughter.

Unless….

"What's up with you giving your dad the cold treatment? You haven't seen him in how long and not even a hello?"

As soon as the questions were out there, I regretted them. Sort of.

Not only was their relationship none of my business, but her expression alone told me I was officially on her shit list and all jokes were off. That didn't mean I wasn't curious. Nor did it mean I wasn't prepared to throw my own none-of-my-business questions back at her.

I wished I was a damn cat because I'd need all nine lives for a chance at surviving the glare she shot my way.

"You know," she started, cutting through the silent tension as we eyed each other, "I researched you when I discovered where I was heading and who was working in the unofficial task force."

Oh, here we go.

I barely held back my eyeroll, wondering what shit she was about to fire my way. Whatever she decided on, I could take it.

"It was brave, what you did in Bangkok. Foolish but brave."

My lips parted before I took control of my reaction.

How the fuck did she know about Bangkok?

Not that I'd ask her that. Instead, I challenged, "Foolish for telling my captain to fuck off and saving the hundred and fifty innocents on a burning ship?" I was mildly curious what point she was making.

A nonchalant shrug preceded her saying, "More like foolish for not making sure he was on the burning ship when it finally went down."

Huh.

"Those charges that finally sent him away were a nice touch, though."

I snorted out a laugh, my shoulders relaxing a little. "Every now and then I have a flair for the creative."

When she flashed me a smile, my gut tightened. I had no idea who her mum was or if Valeria took after her at all, but with that smile alone, she was all Matt.

"Blackthorn," I started, pushing my luck, "not Lucas?"

Her smile dimmed but didn't fade completely. "My mum's."

I bobbed my head while racking my brain, wondering if I'd heard of another Blackthorn before—beyond Valeria's dead name.

"Mum was a curator for Sydney Museum,"

Valeria began without prompting, "and she was an author for a time. She was also an EMT for a decade before I was born."

The way she spoke….

"Things started to go to shit with Dad at Mum's twilight vigil."

Fuck.

I suspected, but there were times I wished I was dead wrong.

Her mum was dead.

I'd parted my lips, prepared to utter words that probably meant jack shit to her, when the clang of keys accompanied by multiple pairs of heavy footsteps stopped me.

Looked like we'd start getting some answers at least, even though the need to discover how things had gone so very wrong between Matt and his daughter buzzed through me.

Fucking priorities, Ethan.

"You want to take the lead, or…?" I let my whispered question trail off. Not only was Valeria an active agent of some sort—sector unknown—but her experience outshone my own. My ego wasn't so big that I didn't know when to hand over the proverbial reins. Sure, I could be a grumpy arsehole, and sometimes I could get in my own way, but in a situation like this, I had no issues following Valeria's lead.

She studied me a beat before nodding just as the door unlocked and bright unnatural light filtered into the concrete room. Did that mean it was night? As soon as the thought hit me, I recalled the conversation about being in the air I overheard during my abduction.

The memory offered a much-needed kick up the arse that this was not the time or the place for the getting-to-know-you fun with Valeria. I relaxed my shoulders despite being on high alert, relieved I was on my knees.

Sure, I was clamped to the ground, but given the opportunity, I'd do some damage.

A large body blocked the light before stepping inside the room. He was tall and built like a brick shithouse. Likely ex-military and definitely a lackey. But something was different. Off.

This man…. I scented the air. Human. He wasn't with Hornell. Wasn't part of the security that had headed to the warehouse where the server was located. For one, all our intel told us Hornell didn't work with humans. Not anymore. Two—

A woman dressed in standard-issue cargo pants and a nondescript black T-shirt appeared in the empty doorway. Vampire.

Valeria gasped.

I snapped my attention her way, tensing at her wide eyes and her pale face. She knew this—

"Mum?"

My head turned so quickly, the crack of my neck echoed around the room. *Mum?*

What the hell was it with these Aussie vamps and their dramatic disclosures? Talk about a mind fuck.

The twists just kept on coming. One minute it was all "oh yeah, she's dea—

Then *bam*—psych!

CHAPTER 7

LUCAS

Ice cut through my veins.

By the time we'd reached the old water station, it had been rendered impossible to enter. Flames had engulfed the building. Within ten minutes, the roof at the front of the building had caved in, leaving me pacing, tugging at the short strands of my hair, while searching for any signs of Valeria and Ethan.

That the fire crew indicated a while later that the building was empty came as a relief. That panic didn't truly fade, though. How could it when it meant almost two hours had passed since their disappearance?

That was two hours where they could have reached any number of locations.

But it was Durrant's calm, almost detached voice that caused the shards of ice.

"What do you mean you can't pull anyone in to help?"

For years I'd given my all, my everything, even gone so far as to isolate myself from my daughter, mostly in the name of protecting my country.

"I'll do what I can, Matt. You know I will. But with Hornell not at the location in Melbourne, it's put us on high alert. We have the Sydney and Canberra teams processing everything we gathered and the arrests we made. But that's opened up a whole new network of intel. We need to act now to shut everything down and keep on Hornell's trail. We're so close and have him on the run."

The vein in my neck pulsed, my jaw tight, my molars grinding.

"We've been able to take down the alerts for your arrests. The team is in the clear." Sympathy crept into her voice, but I wasn't interested.

I needed my daughter and Ethan now. Needed their location. Needed to get them out of whatever nightmare they'd been thrown into.

"And what if this *is* Hornell?" I argued, but I knew it would fall on deaf ears.

The only lead we had indicated that the team who'd infiltrated were not affiliated with Hornell. The confirmation had been a blow as much as it was a relief. If it weren't for the fact that I'd discovered the information, following the trail that took me to the ShadowNet and a job bid for a grab-and-go, which was definitely not Hornell's style, I would have continued to doubt the validity.

But I couldn't. We both knew it.

That didn't help my situation here.

"Dharrun's working with local agents on those individuals they took into custody at the server's location," Durrant said unnecessarily.

I knew the facts. Knew everyone's roles.

Once we'd subdued the assailants in the SUVs, Valeria had already left the scene on Alinta's orders. Misplaced relief had flooded me when I'd watched her drive away, my gratitude following, since Alinta had gotten Valeria out of there. We'd all expected to have to run, to take cover. Everyone except for Tarka, who'd had a team on standby.

Something I would have been pissed about since I hadn't known about it. Considering they'd arrived in the nick of time, I didn't have it in me to be frustrated at being left in the dark.

They'd raced in, helping us to take down those on Hornell's payroll. Not everyone had been killed, but I wished they had. It would have at least freed up Dharrun and Alinta.

"You have Tarka. He's agreed to help, right?" Durrant said, cutting through my thoughts.

I did, thankfully.

He had no jurisdiction, considering he was no longer an agent, and he'd already said he and his men would assist, but that wasn't the point. Sure, Ethan didn't work for the SICB either. He wasn't even Australian. But he had gone above and beyond to help us.

Then there was my daughter, who still worked for the government, yet Durrant couldn't offer anything?

My head swirled with frustration, building and expanding, threatening to overwhelm and incapacitate if I wasn't careful.

"Matt, I'm sorry. As soon as I can free up Kent, she's yours."

"Fine." I cut the call, unable to deal with pleasantries. Shoving my phone into my pocket, I concentrated on my heartbeat, focussed on slowing it down and pulling myself together. Both Valeria and Ethan needed me on my game. Not a chance I could let them down.

With one last breath, I squared my shoulders and turned, heading towards the two waiting SUVs Tarka's men had saved our arses in. Tarka stopped talking, his gaze on me as soon as I stepped close. At the unasked question in his eyes, I shook my head.

He nodded once, turned to a wolf shifter called Hannah, and instructed, "We're going to head out now and meet at the airport base. You go ahead and set up. We'll be five minutes behind."

With a nod, she gathered a couple of bags before she and three members of their team jumped into one of the SUVs, leaving the other for me and Tarka.

"Airport?" I asked immediately. Did that mean he had some new information?

The shift was so minute, I suspected many would miss it. But not only did I know Tarka well, my training went above and beyond tech development.

"What is it?" I pressed.

"Jump in. We're going to need some privacy."

If my heart could hammer as fast, it would be beating at the speed of a bullet train. My stomach hollowed as I quickly got into the passenger seat, turning expectantly towards Tarka when he entered and switched on the engine.

"Belt up." He pulled away from the kerb, heading in the same direction as his team.

Holding back my building frustration, I did so, not wanting any more delays on whatever he was about to lay on me.

"One of our guys is a tech whizz. I'd say a few more years and he'll be on your level."

Understanding the implication, I nodded. He needed me to trust the intel and the source. "Go on."

He flicked me a glance; this time, his expression

told me exactly what he was feeling. Concern. Anguish. Sympathy.

Unable to control my fear, "Is it Valeria?" spilled out. I needed to know. I couldn't handle the potentially earth-shattering news being drawn out any further.

"As far as we know, she's okay. We've no reason to believe otherwise."

I rubbed at my chest, absorbing his words, welcoming the relief even if it was likely to be short-lived. "So, what is it? What's going on?"

He pulled onto the motorway, sparing me a glance before saying, "We're waiting for a location, but we think we're close to a lead."

This was good. Better than I hoped for without my own team here to assist.

"Tell me about Maya's death."

I froze, my mind whiting out in surprise. *Maya?* Struggling to form words as my brain tried to put together what he was really asking, I simply gaped, brows drawn low in a frown.

When I didn't respond, he took a beat, gaze roaming my face. With a slow, heavy exhale, Tarka shook his head. "Matt, we think Maya's alive."

I latched on to the door, my stomach churning, my mind buzzing. I scrambled for the handle, not making sense of Tarka's panicked words or exactly what I was doing.

I needed to get out. Needed air.

Needed to be out of this car before I threw up.

I jolted in my seat as the car jerked to a stop. Not hesitating, I scrambled for the door and practically fell out. Bent double, I heaved as white flecks danced in my vision, blurring my view. I heaved again, nothing but bile creeping its way up my throat.

Blood pounded in my ears. Despite the noise, my thoughts bled through thick and fast.

Impossible. She can't be. How? No, it can't be true.

I shook my head, eyes burning, sweat beading on my skin.

She was dead. She had to be. The thought of her still being alive, sharing the same space as me, breathing the same air—

Valeria.

"Fuck, Valeria." I bolted upright and turned in panic, smacking into Tarka's broad chest.

His large hands gripped my shoulders, his voice soothing as he said, "If Valeria is with Maya, she'll be okay."

I shook my head, finally meeting his gaze. "She won't be. This is Maya we're talking about."

When he winced, I just knew he was remembering, knew he recalled the moment when he realised the true extent of Maya's deception… how toxic and damn evil she was.

My external scars may have healed, but he'd been the one to come to my rescue. He'd witnessed the fallout, the battle, my recovery, how I'd protected Valeria.

"Fuck." The word punched out of him, and as quickly as he'd originally held on to me, he released me, racing back to the door of the vehicle.

I followed suit. The need to get to Valeria and protect her overtook my instinct to hide, to cower. I loathed the reaction, despised it, and had hoped to never feel that way again.

And Ethan. I closed my eyes as Tarka pulled out into traffic, ignoring the horns and screech of brakes. If Maya knew Ethan meant something to me, who knew what she'd do.

The woman couldn't be trusted.

"How sure are you?" I finally asked. Information, the facts, getting as much as possible would help me keep my sanity. With intel, I could plan and strategize. That would be the only way to get through this.

"I know it's not what you want to hear, but let us get to the airport, and we should have some answers soon."

"So fairly fucking sure, then?" I snapped, then immediately clamped my mouth shut and ran a hand over my face. "Sorry." Anxiety pulled on the threads of my control.

Ignoring my outburst, he asked, "Maya's death. Tell me about it."

I glanced his way. "You know the official report." There was nothing to add to it.

He was one of the few who'd had clearance, and only because of his relationship with me and that he'd stumbled on the fallout.

He bobbed his head. "Maya Blackthorn, Supernatural Intelligence Agency covert operative for twenty-nine years. Six months before her reported death—an explosion during a joint force takedown in Darwin—intel indicated she was a double agent working for the North Koreans."

I glanced out the window, recalling the moment I'd discovered not only that she was an SIA operative and not a curator, but that she was also a spy—though not for Australia.

A dull ache formed in my chest. The humiliation, the fear, the anger, *every* emotion, then add in the years of accepting her narcissistic behaviour, her gaslighting—it had almost been too much. Only Valeria had kept me together—the need to keep her safe and protect her from the truth was the driving force to doing whatever it took to take Maya down.

Had my heart broken?

Maybe a fraction of it. But it had been a long time since I'd loved Maya.

Voice strained, Tarka continued, "It was three months into the active investigation into Maya when I was read in. That was the night I found you beaten within an inch of your life."

I swallowed hard and risked a glance. He was a good friend, the best. Shame hit me that it had been so long since we'd seen each other.

"Don't look at me like that."

My brows shot high. "Like what?"

"I understand why you kept your distance."

I winced. "That doesn't make it okay."

"It does."

I wasn't sure I agreed, but I appreciated he understood. Just seeing him, despite all he'd done to save me and help protect Valeria, brought back the years of mental abuse I'd suffered as well as the memories of the attack Maya orchestrated and bore witness to once she discovered I knew her real identity and the extent of her deception.

That had been three months before the SICB and SIA had located her and obliterated the weapons lab she'd been stowed away in. Given the heat and the destruction, the remains had been impossible to identify.

I had witnessed her entering the building with

my own two eyes, as had the task force. There'd also been her Tungsten ring discovered in the rubble. A family heirloom, she'd told me. Once we had access to the damaged ring, we discovered its more nefarious function.

The ring wasn't just a piece of jewellery; it was a deadly weapon in itself—a highly advanced technological device. Its function was to siphon the vital signs and biometric data of whomever she pressed it against.

I remembered the shock we felt when we realised its true purpose. Maya had been using it to gather intelligence on the agents in the SIA and SICB, as well as other government officials, exploiting their vulnerabilities and weaknesses while leaving a trail of death and destruction in her wake.

It was the latter that had been all too easy to discover once we'd started digging.

Even now, recalling the discovery sent shivers down my spine. It was a reminder of how deeply Maya had been involved in the sinister world of espionage and the danger she had posed to everyone around her.

"You doing okay?"

I nodded, trying not to wallow in the guilt that weighed me down when I thought about Maya.

Rationally—and with therapy—I knew her ability

to manipulate was out of my control. For hours, days, and weeks, I'd berated myself, certain that if I'd left at the first red flag—the first time she'd lashed out with her tongue, threatened to take Valeria away from me—the fallout wouldn't have been so awful. She'd rendered me weak, incapacitated, and incapable. Made me believe I couldn't do my job—not without running things by her first.

Then there was Valeria. The hot and cold Maya blew towards her—something I'd fiercely tried to protect my daughter from.

"I will be when we have Valeria and Ethan," I finally replied.

We reached the secure gate for the private hangar. After passing through security, Tarka drove towards one of the plane hangars, casting me a brief look before asking, "You and Ethan. Am I right in thinking there's something beyond professional between you?"

What I wanted to do was close my eyes, sag into my chair, and wave a magic wand to make all this go away. Instead, a question about Ethan and me had been thrown my way, one I wasn't sure how to answer.

We'd known each other for a little over a week,. That was barely a breath in my long life. But he was the first person since Maya that I'd let in—both emotionally and sexually. Why I trusted him, I hadn't pulled apart fully. But I did.

And after years of being lied to and manipulated, that I did trust him was a miracle in itself.

"Yes." My reply was short and to the point. I couldn't explain beyond that.

"Okay." We pulled up inside the hangar, the late-morning sun cutting off abruptly. "When can you get access to your team?"

Technically Tarka should know nothing about them, considering our covert credentials. The moment I realised Valeria was missing, the function of my team had been the first thing I'd divulged.

He needed all the facts to know what he could be dealing with.

Though if this was all Maya, then it was absolutely personal.

"I'm not sure. Durrant insisted they continue the mission to locate Hornell." Frustration twisted my gut. I wanted that too. Needed Hornell put away. But Kent and my team, Callen… they were family.

"Do they know about Maya?"

The question was a smack in the face and a sneer at my thoughts of "family," considering only Kent knew about Valeria's existence.

"No."

Unclipping his belt, he angled towards me. "Maybe it's time you started letting people in."

I didn't have it in me to laugh, but how I wanted to do so, scoff off my struggle to do just that.

Then why had I let Ethan in? Twelve hours ago, I could have tried fooling myself by blaming our recklessness on the impermanence of our connection, but something more was there.

My team had my back. Always. But opening up fully would reveal the mess and chaos of my world. That would mean I'd have to deal with it… eventually. And letting them in, sharing my burdens, meant I'd leave myself vulnerable. Staying in control and relying on myself kept me safe and busy and stopped me from spiralling.

My throat thickened at the very thought. But what other choice did I have?

I settled on "Maybe."

Nodding his acceptance, Tarka exited the car. I was hot on his heels.

There might have been a whirlwind of unknown, but this I could handle. The alternative was not worth considering.

The slam of the car doors echoed around the large hangar. I took it all in as I headed towards where Tarka's crew had set up a small but impressive workstation.

The hangar was expansive, with high ceilings and walls lined with various tools and equipment neatly organised on racks. The faint scent of aviation fuel mixed with the metallic tang of machinery tickled my nose, while fluorescent lights hummed overhead, casting a bright glow over the space.

At the centre of the hangar sat a sleek private jet, its polished exterior gleaming under the lights. My eyes widened. Just how successful was Tarka? The man had been keeping secrets.

Tarka's crew moved with precision around the plane, loading supplies and checking equipment. Two members were focused intently on computer screens, likely gathering and analysing data, while another member coordinated over a headset, speaking in terse, efficient tones.

The workstation they had set up nearby was equipped with monitors displaying various surveillance feeds and maps. Papers were spread over a table. I stepped closer, targeting the files, and gathered them up. Reading through every piece of information even as I walked, my pulse jumped. The papers detailed intel regarding the abduction of my daughter and Ethan, the man who had become a thorn in my side and left his mark on my heart.

"Where did this flight go?" I picked up the papers that outlined an uncharted flight. How they got the details was neither here nor there. "Do you have information on who was on board?"

Looking briefly at Tarka, Hannah waited for a barely perceptible nod before turning to me and handing me printouts. "These were taken a little over two hours ago. These are from satellite footage over at the Traveston pad."

Dread sat heavily in the pit of my stomach. Looking at this would mean confirmation. Needing a second to prepare myself, I asked, "A helipad close by?"

"Yeah, about fifteen klicks from the warehouse you were targeting."

Surprise had my brows shooting high, and I angled a look at Tarka. With folded arms, the man didn't look the least bit concerned he was sharing illegally obtained footage from satellites he definitely shouldn't have access to. He quirked his brow, and one side of his mouth lifted high.

I shook my head, his arrogance and I-don't-give-a-shit attitude drawing a snort out of me. If not following the law helped me find Valeria and Ethan, I didn't give a damn. It was funny how that worked out. My moral high ground would be completely eviscerated by the time this was over.

Perhaps I should be more concerned about that than I was.

No longer allowing the distraction to pull me from the image, I took a look.

The first photo showed Ethan, hog-tied and his head lolling to the side. Two large men appeared to be about to put him in the helicopter. A Sikorsky UH-60 Black Hawk. Scrunching my brow, I glanced at Tarka. "Do you know of any UH-60s in Australia? I thought we only had S-70A-9s and MH-60Rs."

A grin pulled his lips high, excitement sparking in his eyes. "And that is how we're going to track the bastards."

Hope bloomed in my chest, but it quickly froze when I looked at the second photo.

Valeria.

Anger surged in its place. My daughter appeared unconscious and was also bound at her wrists and ankles. She was thrown over a man's shoulder, the frame capturing Valeria being relocated to the helicopter.

"How close are we to finding their location?"

"Maybe thirty minutes," Hannah responded.

I closed my eyes. That was too long. They were already hours ahead.

"I need you to take a look at this." Tarka's tone, calm and gruff, pulled at me.

When I opened my eyes, he indicated one of the screens and tugged out the chair in front of it. I sat willingly, appreciating the familiarity of being at a computer. Here I felt in control. "What do you need?"

I PEERED OUT AT THE SKYLINE, TAKING IN THE CITYSCAPE of Melbourne emerging through the dense rain clouds. The towering skyscrapers pierced the misty shroud, their silhouettes softened by the steady drizzle. The Yarra River wound its way through the city, its surface rippling under the weight of the downpour.

As we descended lower, the streets below glistened with rain, traffic moving steadily despite the wet conditions. Meanwhile, I held myself tightly, refusing to tap my foot. Three more minutes and we'd be on the tarmac of the small private airstrip. Three more minutes and we'd be heading north out of the city, each kilometre we travelled taking me closer to Valeria and Ethan.

The rain-slicked windows distorted the view, giving the city an almost surreal quality, but even through the dreariness, the plane descended smoothly. I gripped the armrests, barely listening to the conversation between Tarka and Liam. All I needed was to be off the plane and in the car.

Tarka's "No one's left the site" grabbed my attention. With his gaze on me, he offered an up-nod as I managed a relieved smile.

There were seventy kilometres between me and my girl, and with eyes in the sky, Tarka remained confident that was still the case. Having that confirmation helped the final couple of minutes pass by.

It helped to not think about the unknown. There'd been no contact from Maya. No threats or ransom notes. No demands.

One thing we were all now certain of was that Maya was responsible. That knowledge should have had me calling Durrant immediately, yet I hadn't. Tarka and I had a plan. Durrant coming in now, getting the SIA involved, would hinder that. Their priority would undoubtedly be capturing Maya or possibly making a second attempt at wiping her off the face of the earth.

Not a chance I'd put Valeria or Ethan at risk like that.

As soon as the wheels were down, we were up and grabbing our gear, ready to dive out of the plane and jump into the waiting cars.

Tarka sidled up to me, his voice taking on a friendly lilt. "You know, when all this is over, there's always room for you and whoever you trust on the team."

I angled a glance his way.

"It has its perks, working in security."

A small smile pulled at my lips. "It does appear lucrative." I arched my brow. "I always figured you'd find your feet when you jumped ship."

"Damn straight." He chuckled, his large hand clamping on my shoulder and squeezing lightly. My gut clenched at the gesture, as it reminded me of Ethan. "But in all seriousness, think about it."

I studied his expression as the engines powered down. "I'll think about it." I just didn't know how I felt about the possibility of leaving the SICB. Just the thought of the break in my routine, not having so much to focus on that would keep me distracted, put me on the cusp of a cold sweat breaking out.

The single cabin crew aboard the plane opened the door, and the stairs descended. This really was a fancy-arse plane. Sure, I'd made a tidy sum over the years with my tech and could likely afford maybe a helo, but something as ostentatious as this? I suspected not.

"Head towards hangar D," Tarka instructed as we exited, the drizzle quickly coating our faces and shoulders. "Let's get loaded up fast, and we'll head out. No pit stops."

Good, this was all good.

With a bag in each hand, I focussed forwards and

on the sign for hangar D. Voices rippled around the metal hangar. With the car engines running, it was difficult to pick up individual words, let alone distinct voices.

Five SUVs waited. Seven of us had arrived from Brisbane, and Tarka had organised a unit to meet us here. I rounded the first vehicle, stopping dead in my tracks. Kent, her arms folded and looking pissed at whatever Callen was laughing at, leaned against the black Jeep. Her gaze snapped to mine, relief swirling in her green depths until she shuttered her reaction.

Callen's laughter died, and in two steps, he snatched me up and wrapped me in a fierce hug.

Kent had told him. I'd given her permission in the short call I'd made before the flight, providing her a brief rundown and access to a private server so she could discover the truth about Maya.

"Fuck, man…." He petered off, hugging me even harder until, apparently, he needed to check for himself that I was okay. He held me at arm's length, eyes roaming.

"I'm fine." I rolled my eyes but didn't shrug him away. We'd worked together for a long time, and this was just what he did. He loved hard and fiercely.

"But you were in a gunfight. A. Gun. Fight. Shit, did you even remember how to turn the safety off?"

A deep, familiar chuckle reached me. Michaels.

He threw me a wink as I managed to escape Callen's attention. "You okay there, boss?"

A quick swallow of the bubble of emotions and I nodded. "Yeah." I peered around, taking in Smythe, Shaw, and Chris, and even Hart. "You're all here."

"Fuck, he must have hit his head. Done some damage." Callen stared at me with wide-eyed amusement, completely taking the piss. "There's no other explanation for you to think, for one second, that if you needed us, we wouldn't come running."

"Callen." Kent's tone was all exasperation. "Get out of the man's way so we can make a move."

"Right, we have my *niece* to save and a former psycho ex to take down." Callen rubbed his hands together, an expression of such intense belief sprinkled with joy and determination pouring off him that, damn him, I stepped into his space and hugged him hard.

A huff of surprise preceded his arms squeezing me back.

"We've got you, Lucas." Sincerity bled through his words, shooting warmth into my chest.

I believed him. Believed them all.

And they'd come here for me. To support me.

"Okay." I nodded and stepped back, pulling myself together as best as I could. "Team, roll out."

My unit patted me on the back as they split and

jumped into the vehicles Tarka had supplied, Shaw's "Did Lucas just quote Optimus Prime?" disappearing behind his closed door.

I huffed out a laugh, relief fuelling the action. After I finished the brief introductions between Tarka and my unit, I got behind the wheel of the SUV, Tarka, Kent, and Callen joining me. Driving would help me focus. I needed that more than anything.

In the quiet of the car, the electric engine was whisper soft as we sped out of the hangar, straight through the security check, and onto the road. The rain had slowed, making it easier to navigate through the awful traffic.

Gathering my thoughts, I tried to figure out where to start and what to say.

Considering Callen was with me, I should have known I didn't need to worry. He may have been a bit of a wild card at times, but officially, he was my boss as division leader. Durrant's choice had surprised a lot of people, I was sure—especially Callen when he'd been promoted.

But not me.

He was funny and ridiculous and talked so much shit that sometimes I wanted to throttle him, but his skill was impressive, his determination even more so. Even though he played it down, he was also super smart. Maybe not on the same level with tech like me or computers and programming like Kent and Smythe, but he could read a situation and configure a plan within moments.

More importantly, he earned respect wherever he went. It kind of blew lots of folks' minds, since he could be as irresponsible as a squirrel on a sugar high. While we had exactly zero squirrels in Australia, he more than made up for it.

There was that one time he tried to prove that a paperclip and a rubber band could replace standard-issue handcuffs during an important briefing. Spoiler alert: it didn't work. *Go figure.* But somehow, amid the chaos and the random bursts of interpretive dance that he insisted were "team-building exercises," he managed to command a room like nobody else.

So, despite his quirks and the occasional desire to strangle him with his own tie—which I admittedly only saw him wear once, and for maybe five minutes —Callen was the leader we didn't know we needed. And really, who else could pull off a tactical mission in a Hawaiian shirt and still get results?

Not that he was wearing one now, thank goodness, but the sentiment remained.

"Fifty-word recaps from everyone. I'll start. Kent, you count."

"For the love of a plastic bag." Kent sighed, her fingers twitching. I wasn't sure if it was because she was imagining suffocating Callen, or if it was the fact that she was out in the wild with the rest of us rather than doing damage behind a computer screen.

It was likely both.

Pointedly ignoring Kent, Callen dove straight in. "Here's the lowdown: Durrant's more annoyed than a koala with a hangover. Apparently, we're this close"—he held up his hand so we could see his fore-finger and thumb were barely a millimetre apart—"to having a new warrant out for our arrest."

His grin implied he wasn't in the least bit concerned about this. I could only hope he was exaggerating. Honestly, I couldn't be a hundred percent sure with Callen.

"And no, we still haven't captured Hornell. But… and this is pretty fucking awesome—we snagged his second in command! Which is news to everyone because no one even knew Hornell had a second in command."

How he could sound so gleeful, as if this was an exciting development, was beyond me. He wanted Hornell at the end of a barrel as much as every single member of our unit did.

"Oh, and you'll never guess where he definitely is. Victoria, for sure, but not Melbourne like we assumed. Cray-cray, right?"

Cray-cray? For the love of all that was sacred and whatever deity offered willpower and strength.

"Anyway, we used that 'intel'"—he totally did air quotes—"to convince Durrant we're on top of things and that we should all head here to participate in Hornell-capturing badassery. Technically, we lied, because we have maybe half a clue where he is, but hey, it's the thought that counts, right?"

I sighed, gripping the steering wheel tighter. "Callen, that was way more than fifty words." Apparently, that was all that was important right now. The rest of it was too much on top of everything else I was juggling.

Callen shrugged, undeterred. "Also, Lucas, I've been thinking—if anything ever happens to you, I think Thatch and I should be the legal guardian to the niece we never knew we had. We're doing a stellar job with Lucinda. Valeria could learn the art of tactical kickassery from the best."

Kent, who was in the rear passenger seat, looked up from her laptop—when she'd pulled that out, I had no clue—eyebrow raised. "You do realise she's older than you, right?"

Callen paused, clearly unperturbed. "Age is just a number, Kent."

"And a trained agent in on a whole heap of top-secret shit that would make your head spin."

"Pur-lease, as if she's broken half of the rules I have. There's a whole new skill set right there, just waiting for me to share."

"Says our *boss*." Kent shook her head before refocussing on her screen.

My lips twitched. I appreciated the break in tension. How it was possible I'd missed these guys so much was beyond me. It was probable I needed to get out more.

At my side, Tarka chuckled. "You know that offer I made?"

I side-eyed him.

"I think I may need to add stipulations."

I huffed out a laugh.

"Why do I have a feeling that was a dig at me?" Callen's narrowed gaze met mine through the rearview mirror. He could scowl all he wanted. Both Kent and I knew he was full of shit. The very thought of being the centre of attention made him come alive.

"When Valeria was a kid, she used to want to be a puppy. That's something you could probably help her with." The memory of my seven-year-old obsessed with puppies, going so far as lapping at both water and blood from a bowl on the floor, pushed a smile to my lips. It was quickly erased by a stab of reality.

Right now, this very second, she could be being tortured. Dead.

"Hey." Callen gripped my shoulder from behind, his ability to read the shift in my emotions so swift, I was sure even Tarka would begin to see why he'd earned his role as division leader. "We'll get her back, and we'll buy her a damn puppy if need be."

A sad smile formed as I nodded.

It had been a long time since my child had wanted or needed anything from me.

Not only had I accepted responsibility for her mother "leaving" us after I caused a "car accident" so severe, it resulted in injuries that took me five days to heal from, but I accepted the blame for Maya's "untimely death." The story had been that I'd pushed her mum away as we'd grown apart, and she'd taken a position overseas. Unfortunately, that was where she'd been "caught up in a terrorist attack"—an explosion in the British Museum.

The latter had happened—the explosion had taken many lives, including supes'—shortly after what we'd thought was Maya's actual death in Darwin. It provided the perfect, reasonable explanation to Valeria, Maya's colleagues, and the few friends and family I had left.

I'd kept it all from Valeria—the toxic relationship —when she was a child and when she was just finding her way in the world. Maya's file had been sealed, so regardless of Valeria's position and role, she would never gain access.

Until now.

Callen eased back in his seat, and the conversation ceased as we drove on. I counted each kilometre, my promise to reach Valeria on a loop in my head. Then there was Ethan.

I cracked my neck.

I had to trust that together, they'd be okay. Even without a full explanation and no promises between us, if Ethan was able to protect Valeria, he would in a heartbeat. The certainty pressed against me, warm and growing familiar—something that had been happening more and more over the past week.

Increasing the speed, I watched the speedometer edge towards 130 as we finally broke free from the city and out of suburbia.

We'd make it. Get there in time. For what, I had no idea. But it didn't matter. I'd buried Maya a long time ago, in more ways than one.

I'd do it again in an instant, confident that every person at my side would follow my lead.

CHAPTER 8
WILDER

"Fuck you," I spat, wishing I could shoot lasers out of my eyes.

The wild-eyed psycho brandishing a hot poker simply grinned.

I'd learned a lot—not only about myself, but also Valeria, Maya, and just what Matt had survived.

I'd discovered what burnt flesh smelled like—specifically, my own. After this, there was no way I'd ever be able to eat barbequed pork again. For real, singed skin not only hurt like a fucker, but the stench would likely be with me for weeks.

And I absolutely planned for that to happen. Not a chance I wasn't getting out of here alive, leaving Maya and her sadistic fuckwit team in the ground with bullets in their brains.

I'd never killed for revenge before. Sure, I'd

thought about it a time or two, but up until this point, I didn't think I had it in me. How wrong I was.

What was also clear was that the torture had only just begun, but I still had no idea why.

No questions had been asked. No demands had been made.

Everything about this situation felt wrong. Sure, for the obvious reasons that I'd been captured and made to fucking burn, but still, what was the point of it all?

Before I could tell the lion shifter where he really needed to stick the hot poker, the door opened, revealing the head honcho of psychopaths—Maya.

A sly smile tilted her lips. Objectively, I imagined those attracted to women would be drawn to her. Until they looked into her eyes and saw nothing but bottomless pits of crazy. And that was not a term I threw around for the fun of it.

It had taken a shocked, spiralling Valeria probably five minutes to realise this was not the parent she remembered. While I still didn't know how long ago Maya had been presumed dead, Valeria had definitely been old enough to know her well. But I imagined that version of her mum was nowhere to be seen.

Maya flipping her shit almost immediately had been enough of a red flag for Valeria to be on high alert and recognise the threat the woman was. Her mum then cussing out Matt, threatening his balls and his life, proceeding to vent and rave about the years she'd needed to stay underground and transform and declaring that "they" would all pay, pretty much helped me to understand that all of this info was also news to Valeria.

She'd definitely believed her mum to be not only dead but a museum curator.

Talk about a shock.

Valeria had since been dragged away. She'd managed to put two shifters on the ground, but considering she was restrained and unarmed, her head still foggy, she'd lost the battle.

Ever since she'd been taken away, a ball of dread sat in my gut. It didn't matter her experience or her age. Valeria was Matt's daughter. The need to make sure she was okay burned brightly in the very centre of my being.

Maya's nose wrinkled when she stepped further into the concrete shell of a room. She eyed the fresh burn on my arm, satisfaction alight in her gaze. "I hate not having symmetry, Josiah."

Josiah immediately pulled the poker out of the small cast iron fire they'd wheeled in a while back. The end glowed red.

I stiffened, muscles bunching, preparing for pain.

Searing agony tore through my arm. The heat was instant and all-consuming, spreading through my flesh like wildfire. It felt as though the very essence of my being was being burned away, layer by layer. My skin hissed and crackled, the smell of scorched flesh filling the air, mingling with the acrid scent of the smoke.

I'd heal. Maybe. Unless they continued to burn the same spot over and over again, never giving my body time to rejuvenate.

The pain burrowed deep, sending shockwaves through my nerves, rattling my bones as Josiah continued holding the metal to my flesh. I clenched my teeth, a guttural scream threatening to escape.

Not a chance I'd give either of them the satisfaction.

The moment the poker tore free, I inhaled deeply through my mouth, avoiding the vile stench.

"Much better." Maya nodded in approval, turned, and headed back to the door.

What the fuck?

"Where the hell do you think you're going?" I shouted, ignoring the sweat pouring off me. Calling out to her could be a mistake, but if I had no choice but to sit here and take it, I wanted to at least know why.

She turned slowly on her heel, her eyes like

daggers as they locked on me. A sneer followed, and she took a step away from the door, her roaming gaze making it crystal clear she wasn't impressed with what she saw.

Right back at ya, lady.

Just when I didn't think she was going to respond, she took another step towards me. "You made a mistake coming to Australia. You made a second mistake by not leaving immediately. The third, though." She tutted. A flash of just how unhinged she was appeared in her expression as a cruel smile twisted her lips. "It was the third that landed you here."

Confusion clouded my thoughts.

The hell was she talking about?

What on earth did I have to do with anything going on here? Sure, I'd sucked off her ex. Though, technically, was he really that to her, since she'd lied about who she was in the first place and, for her, their whole relationship was a big, fat lie?

That was one of many snippets of information I'd discovered.

But me sucking off Matt and admittedly beginning to crush on the vampire harder than was sensible could not have anything to do with what—

"I always found going down on Mathew tedious. You didn't have the same problem, right?"

No way in hell could she know that. Any of it. Right? *Fuck.*

And seriously? If this was a weird, fucked-up revenge scheme by a jealous ex, I was going to lose my shit. Who did that? I'd already established that she had some serious mental health issues. I was no doctor, but I didn't think the depth of her mental illness was something that could be managed by tablets or professional support.

I suspected there was a whole brainwashed situation. What was the Red Room's equivalent in North Korea?

But Maya.... When we added in the whole double-agent, traitor-to-her-country thing as well as her sadistic nature.... I sighed, seriously pissed. My shoulders sagged with the reality check.

The revenge and jilted-lover thing perhaps weren't so farfetched for the vampire before me.

The more burning issue was responding to her question. "I'm pretty sure I didn't brush my teeth after swallowing Matt's cum. I loved every second of it." I smiled inwardly when her features tightened.

It wasn't enough to stop me.

"So either you have a voyeurism kink and have managed to find a way to do whatever creepy shit you need to get the old blood pumping, or you're just a bitter, sadistic fuck who can't move on and get a life, so you have to come back like a bad stink. Which is it?"

She moved before I could prepare myself, her fingers grasping my throat and squeezing. The iron grip made it impossible to breathe. My eyes strained, muscles tensed under her grasp. With her face inches from mine, I fought her hold, moving my shoulders to try to break free.

Her strength was impossible, like nothing I'd ever felt before.

Think. I stilled, trying to get my brain to cooperate.

Making eye contact, I stared and took in every piece of detail I could.

Red flecks joined the dark green of her irises, a handful in each but absolutely noticeable and wrong.

So very wrong.

Understanding slammed into me. It would have caught my breath if I'd had access to any oxygen.

Holy shit.

I croaked, "Hor-nell."

Immediately, her grip loosened, and I gasped for air, struggling to suck in enough to get rid of the white spots dancing in my vision.

Standing upright after releasing my neck, Maya peered down at me. Distaste and distrust filled her expression, and while she seemed more in control and lucid, it was a ruse.

"Do you—" I broke into a hacking cough that seared my throat. "Do you work *for* him or *with* him?"

Her eyes narrowed.

"You do, right?" I took a deep breath and cracked my neck side to side, relieved that my raw throat had started to show signs of healing, my voice already less gruff. "I can't see you as someone who'd have an implant, but there's something… one of their cocktails, maybe, pumped right into your vein."

That had to be it.

Vampires didn't have red eyes. Those flecks in hers screamed chemical manipulation.

Something beyond blood and hatred pumped in her veins, and given the way she'd released me after I'd said Hornell's name, it wasn't necessary to be a genius to put two and two together.

Fuck.

A new possibility that became more and more probable as I sat here, tied to the chair, at the very beginning of being tortured, revealed itself.

"You're here for me. Hornell needs me for something." My words were flat as I absorbed their truth. When she remained silent, I pushed, "Is it just happenchance you were the one to come for me, or was it deliberate, since I was with Lucas?"

I couldn't call him Matt. Not with her. Which didn't make any sense, I knew, but nothing about this situation was regular.

Ignoring my questions, she stood before me with her arms folded. "The schematics for the chip. Where are they?"

I ran my tongue over my top teeth. All I needed was to break free from the wrist restraints, and my bear form could take care of the rest. It had taken a long time to tame my wilder instincts, the urges pushing me to relinquish control and give in to my baser needs.

If I stayed here for much longer, it would only be a matter of time before I lost my shit and shifted without full control. It might even be enough to tear me free from the restraints. It wasn't a myth that bears could go berserk. The one time it had happened to me wasn't a memory I liked to recall.

But hell, maybe I needed to succumb and lose control.

If ever a situation called for it, now would be the time.

I just needed the suppression cuffs off first.

Narrow-eyed, Maya studied me, a dangerous mix

of curiosity and disdain in her gaze. I had to provoke her, push her to the edge.

"You think you're in control here, Maya?" I scoffed, a smirk following. "You're just a puppet, strung along by Hornell. Do you even know what his real plans are? Or are you just too doped up to care?"

Fury flashed in her eyes, a muscle in her jaw twitching. She was making this too easy.

"You talk too much," she hissed, stepping closer. "Maybe Josiah needs to remind you of your place."

I smirked, ignoring the sharp pain in my arm from the fresh burn. "Josiah?" I scoffed. Hell, I loved the thrill of pissing people off. I lived for this shit. "The lion who reeks of weakness? He couldn't break me if he tried. But you know that, don't you? You need him to do your dirty work because you're afraid you'll mess up. Again."

She didn't need to know I was grasping at straws. But without a doubt, she wouldn't be here and on whatever drug that buzzed through her system if her life was all hearts and rainbows.

Anger flared in her eyes, and she turned to Josiah. "Make him suffer. And don't hold back this time."

With a nod, Josiah's expression morphed into a mask of grim determination. Maya touched her ear and froze. Interesting. Was she wearing some sort of communication device? Was that Hornell in her ear? "I'll be back. Don't disappoint me."

As she stormed out of the room, I saw my opportunity. Josiah approached, his eyes gleaming with the thrill of the torment he thought he was about to inflict. His mistake was immediate—he moved around to the back of my chair.

Tensing, I waited for the perfect moment. As he reached to grab my shoulder, I slammed my body backwards with all my strength. The chair crashed into his legs, knocking him off balance. He hit the ground hard, a surprised grunt escaping his lips.

Not wasting a second, I threw my head backwards, the back of my skull connecting with his face. Once, twice—until his grip loosened and his body went limp.

With Josiah unconscious on the floor, I manoeuvred my body, contorting to reach the keys dangling from the chain in his pocket. My fingers fumbled, desperation driving me. Finally, I snagged the keys and awkwardly unlocked the cuffs.

The suppression fell away, and a surge of power rushed through me.

Fuck yes.

My form shifted, bones and muscles rearranging as fast as a blink until I stood as a towering bear.

I roared, the sound echoing off the concrete walls.

This room wouldn't contain me. And now, I had one mission: finding Valeria and getting us both out of this hellhole.

Charging out of the room, I followed her scent, my bear instincts guiding me. Valeria was near, and nothing would stand in my way.

Teeth met flesh when I took a wolf down, the guard too focussed on stuffing his face with food to sense me coming. I turned a corner and was greeted by another wolf shifter in human form and… I tilted my head, unsure what I was scenting.

The woman with the odd scent charged at me, not giving me time to think.

That was her first mistake—not going for the gun strapped to her leg. Her second was attempting to grab me in a chokehold. Another roar raged from me as I tore at her arm, the scream ripping free from her more satisfying than it should have been.

I dropped her to the ground, allowing her to crawl away while trying to hold her shoulder in place. Whoever this team was that Maya or Hornell had put together, they were pitifully lacking. What happened back at my capture was piss-poor judgment on my part and pure luck on theirs. It would be the story I'd stick to.

I smacked the gun out of another shifter's hand. A satisfying crack of his bone ricocheted around the corridor. With a grunt, he gripped his arm, leaving him defenceless. He had a choice. I roared again, spittle breaking free and landing on his cheek. Terror seeped from his pores, satisfying the wild flurry under my skin that begged for pain and destruction.

Then he ran, darting in the other direction as fast as his shaky legs could carry him. Maybe some of the individuals in this unit weren't as stupid as I first thought.

I hooked the keys onto one of my claws, hoping they would help offer us a way out of here.

On four legs, I followed Valeria's scent, not coming across any more issues. It was strange for what appeared to be a large facility to have so few guards. Maybe they were only expecting to take me in, and considering my involvement, they didn't think anyone would come after me.

The thought sent a ripple of longing through my thick coat.

Matt would come for his daughter, but a flicker of hope stirred in my chest that just maybe he would come for me too.

Voices alerted me to Maya's presence. Hers was loud, unhinged. I paused. Valeria's calm voice was much quieter in comparison. I listened in.

"... all this time. Did you truly think I'd be interested in anything you had to offer?" Tension pitched

Valeria's voice low. Gone was the initial surprise, the whisper of longing evident in those first couple of minutes.

While Maya had already overshared a lot, from Valeria's tone, I suspected the full extent of her mother's betrayal and maybe the condition of her mental health had been revealed. What concerned me more was how deep Maya was in with Hornell and what types of changes she'd embraced.

I'd only recently started a deep dive into all the experiments and enhancements Hornell was responsible for. Most of my time had been pulled into finding his location, which meant, with Maya's involvement, we may be closer than ever before.

"He's twisted you, turned you away from me." Cruelty matched the venom in Maya's tone.

Valeria scoffed with strained amusement. "Well, at least I know you haven't been spying on me for all these years."

"What's that supposed to mean?"

"If you had, you'd know Dad kept all of this, everything about you, to himself. Even your death, he took respons—"

"He was responsible."

A pregnant pause followed before Valeria, voice tight, said, "That may be the case, but the story he told me was that you were innocent and in the wrong place at the wrong time. I blamed him for your death. Blamed him for your separation and that you died because he forced you to leave."

"If it weren't for Mathew discovering the truth, then we could have been a family. As soon as your training was over, I planned to bring you in." Maya's voice gentled; however, the note of unhinged desperation remained as she continued. "We could have worked together, travelled the world—"

"Doing what? Betraying my country and then sipping a margarita at the poolside? Maybe killing a few innocents when they saw something they shouldn't have and then celebrating by doing some shoe shopping with you? Mu—Maya, you don't know me at all if you think I would betray the agency, let alone hurt Dad."

My gut clenched at her words, but hell if they didn't fill me with relief.

"Then you being here is just a distraction."

The ice in Maya's voice caused goose bumps to ripple along my skin. Barely a second later, I heard the slide of a foot on concrete, and a gurgle tore through the air.

Fuck.

I launched into the room, my gaze landing on a wide-eyed Valeria, who snapped her attention to me. Red misted my vision, a growl tearing free at the blood dripping down Valeria's neck from Maya's nails clawing at her throat.

Maya didn't stop, didn't look my way—whether lost in bloodlust or so ruled by whatever ran through her veins, I didn't know. What I did know was that Valeria's eyes bugged, the whites of her eyes turning red with broken blood vessels.

I darted towards them, my heavy thuds eating up the distance. I swiped out with a strong paw, knocking Maya to the side. The shove released her grip from Valeria's neck, and she quickly gulped in air and coughed painfully.

Jumping to her feet, Maya hissed, the red flecks in her eyes practically glowing. The hell had happened to her?

A shift of her ankle was the only warning I had before she hurled herself at me, fangs extended and her hands outstretched.

I twisted out of the way, preventing her from clawing at my throat. My thick fur offered me some protection, but vampires were strong and wily. Considering I didn't know the full effects of the chemicals that'd been pumped inside her, I couldn't take anything for granted.

"Don't... kill h-er," Valeria croaked.

The words barely penetrated, but I knew she was right. With the likelihood that Hornell's voice was in her ear, we couldn't afford for her to die. Plus, taking out this woman—Valeria's mum and Matt's ex—was not something I wanted on my conscience. Way to put a strain on a relationship before it had even begun.

Maya's movements were a blur, and the next instant, she was on top of me, her weight surprisingly light but her strength monstrous. I rolled to the side, using the momentum to throw her off balance. She landed with a hiss, baring her fangs at me, a deranged glint in her eyes.

I roared, my voice deep and guttural in my bear form, the keys still hooked around one of my claws.

Maya lunged again, faster than I anticipated. Her sharp nails raked my side, and pain flared up my ribs. I retaliated with a powerful swipe, aiming for her legs. She leapt back, evading my attack by a hair's breadth.

"You won't stop me," Maya spat, circling me like a predator.

I growled, focussing on her movements. She was quick, too quick, but I had brute strength on my side. I needed to incapacitate her, not kill her. My mind raced, thinking of ways to bring her down without ending her life. The keys jingled softly with my movements, a constant reminder of what I had to do.

Maya darted forwards, aiming for my eyes. I

reared up on my hind legs, towering over her, and brought my paws down with thunderous force. She twisted midair, avoiding a direct hit, but the impact sent her sprawling across the floor.

I glanced quickly at Valeria, who was struggling against her restraints, her face pale, her expression livid. The keys. I needed to get the keys to her.

Maya hissed, realising my distraction, and pushed off the ground to launch herself at me with deadly intent. My heart lurched, and I threw myself in her path, catching her midleap. We tumbled to the ground in a tangle of limbs and fur.

She writhed and snarled beneath me, her claws tearing into my flesh. Ignoring the pain, I tightened my grip, pinning her arms to her sides. Maya screamed, a sound filled with fury and desperation.

With a sudden burst of strength, I rolled, flipping Maya off me and sending her crashing into the wall. I used the brief respite to twist my paw, the keys sliding away and skidding across the floor towards Valeria. She reached out with her foot, pulling the keys closer.

Maya roared, fury and frustration clear in her red-tinted eyes as she scrambled to her feet. She charged at me, but I met her with a forceful swipe, knocking her back again. Not a chance I'd let her take me or her daughter down.

I growled, positioning myself between her and Valeria.

On her back on the cold concrete, Valeria fumbled with the keys. "Almost there," she murmured, the sound barely audible over the chaos.

Maya's eyes flickered to Valeria, then back to me. She was calculating, looking for any opening. But I wouldn't give her one. I had to buy Valeria more time.

With a primal roar, Maya launched herself at me once more. I braced myself, my muscles coiling as I prepared to meet her attack. She was relentless, her claws and fangs a blur of motion. I countered every strike, my bear form giving me the strength to withstand her assault.

Behind me, I heard the click of the cuffs opening. Valeria was free.

"Got it!" Valeria shouted, her voice filled with determination.

Maya's eyes widened, and she made a desperate move to get past me. I blocked her path, using my massive bulk to shield Valeria. I roared again, swiping at Maya with all my strength.

Valeria lunged forwards with the chain she'd been tied with and looped it around Maya's legs. She pulled tight, using her full weight to bring the vampire down. Maya thrashed, her screams echoing through the room, but Valeria's effort combined with mine was too much.

With a final, powerful heave, we bound Maya's arms and legs, securing her to the ground. She lay there, panting and defeated, her eyes still burning with hatred.

"It's over, Maya," Valeria said, her voice heartbreakingly neutral.

She glared at her daughter, her chest heaving with exertion. "This isn't over."

Valeria didn't respond and looked at me.

With a nod, I eased back, preparing to shift. I did so immediately, turning back to my human form. The sting on my side had me glancing down. The wound remained open, but the blood flow had slowed.

"Her ear—check the communication device," I said quickly.

Immediately Maya struggled. Before I could suggest gagging her, Valeria raised a fist and punched Maya hard. Out cold, her head flopped to the right, her eyes shutting.

"That'll do it," I said, my brows shooting high. "Remind me not to get on your bad side."

Valeria smirked as she pulled a small device from Maya's ear. "A few hours ago, I would have said the chance of me knocking you out was high."

"And now?"

"Well, one, no way am I touching you while you're naked. I'd say I didn't know where you've been, but since I can scent my dad on you… eww."

Heat flushed my cheeks with the speed of a wildfire racing through dry brush. The fact that she'd rendered me speechless and flustered with mortification was ridiculously impressive.

A huff of laugh preceded her saying, "And two, you just saved my bacon. It kinda means I owe you."

"How about you just promise to not mention what you can scent on me or your dad again and we call us even?"

With a smirk, she nodded. "Deal." Her assessing gaze turned to the small earpiece. "This is a DR76 model." Her lips tilted up as she peered at me.

"No mic." I bobbed my head in relief. Whoever was on the other end at least hadn't heard anything. With that thought, I glanced around the room.

"There are no cameras in here."

I huffed out a tired laugh, ignoring the discomfort at my side. "You're a mind reader?"

She shrugged, the movement casual, but when she angled her neck, it drew my attention there. It looked raw and sore, but the small cuts were already healing.

"Trained operative, remember? I know my shit."

I tilted my head at her. "That you do."

"Is the rest of the building clear?" she asked after a beat.

"Between where I was being kept and here, yes. I didn't get around everywhere. I don't hear anything, though." I listened carefully to double-check. Satisfied all was quiet in the immediate area around us, I considered our options. I needed clothes, and we had to secure Maya properly.

We also needed to trace the signal from the earpiece.

I glanced at the metal loop in the floor that had been used to keep Valeria in place. "Shall we move her while we figure out where we are and how to reach out to Matt?"

Valeria glanced at the hook and nodded even as her muscles became taut at the mention of her dad.

Sympathy surged in my chest.

I had no doubt Matt had tried to do what was right by protecting her from the truth, but I suspected as far as Valeria was concerned, it was the wrong call to make. They had a lot of healing to do. I just hoped they could get things figured out and rebuild their relationship.

"Hey." I waited for her to look at me. When she made eye contact, I said, "You're going to be okay."

Rather than telling me where to shove my opinion, she offered a stiff nod before she stood, grabbed her mum's arm, and dragged her towards the loop in the floor.

We set to work restraining Maya. Once we were confident she wasn't going anywhere, I ducked out to find some clothes, picking up the gun from the floor one of the guards had left behind as I went. After a quick search, I found a stash of clothes in a locker room. The tee was tight, and I couldn't fasten the button at the waist of the jeans, but at least my junk was concealed.

I gave up on looking for shoes, my size 13 feet making it a struggle to squeeze into anything. I debated the pair of sliders I saw, but should I need to run, I'd just end up falling flat on my face.

By the time I made it back to Valeria, the redness on her throat had lessened, and she was on a laptop that she must have found from an adjoining room.

Maya remained unconscious. I hadn't thought she'd been decked so hard. Valeria must have had a stronger right hook than I thought.

"All good?" I asked.

"Yeah. I've just found the access to their security, which is pretty non-existent."

"Really? That doesn't make sense."

"That's what I thought. I kinda figured this location was last minute."

That made some sense. "I haven't ventured for

the exit yet." Which I probably should have. At least two guards that I knew of had made a run for it. They might have called in the cavalry, but my gut and their lack of dedication suggested that wasn't the case. They were hired hands and couldn't have been paid much considering their lack of skills and how quickly they'd been taken out or run for it.

"No need. There's one single camera on the entrance."

"Have you figured out where we are?" I hadn't seen a single window to peer out of.

"Coordinates tell me north of Melbourne."

My brows shot high. "We're in Victoria?" Shit, I must have been dosed up pretty darn good to have missed the whole flight.

"On a tour of Australia, yet you've slept through most of it. That's pretty pathetic."

At her teasing, I grinned. "I'm not sure Australia likes me very much. Everywhere I go, I'm either being punched, shot, or maimed."

A huff of snorting laughter escaped her. She'd parted her lips to speak when an explosion shook the walls around us.

I slammed into Valeria with a grunt, taking her to the floor and covering her with my body to protect her from any debris that may come flying this way.

"Fuck. You're heavy," she groaned as the sound of the explosion settled.

Pounding feet echoing down the corridor replaced the ringing in my ears. I tensed, reluctantly moving an inch to give Valeria space to breathe.

"Any time now, you can move," she groused.

I frowned, wondering why the hell she was giving away our position. I angled, scenting the air. A sneeze followed when concrete dust tickled my nose.

Fuck it all to hell. Looked like my attempt to be stealthy was just as shit as hers.

"It's Dad." She sighed.

My brows shot high as I sniffed again, this time drawing in the scent of gumtrees and vampire. Matt.

Shit, and here I was squashing his daughter.

Before I could move, footsteps screeched to a halt in the open doorway, and I turned to look, seeing the man who I struggled to keep out of my thoughts appear.

His gaze was on mine, assessing, relief evident before his gaze dipped, taking in my position.

"In my defence, you were the one who thought it was a great idea to blow the shit out of a door rather than turning the handle," I said quickly. I eased off a huffing Valeria, shaking off the slivers of plaster and dust. Fortunately, the room remained pretty much intact.

Once on my bare feet, I reached for Valeria. She took my hand immediately, shaking her head, amusement in her gaze as she looked at me. When her focus turned to Matt, she froze, concern morphing her expression. I followed her line of sight, my body locking up.

Ghostly pale, Matt's eyes were wide with fear and horror as he looked to the side. My gaze followed his, landing on the figure on the ground, unconscious but very much alive—his ex-wife. The woman he'd thought was dead.

Her presence looked like it had shaken his world to its core. I wanted nothing more than to go to him, wrap him up in my arms, and hold him close, reassure him he didn't have to do this alone. But before I could say or do anything, more footsteps echoed through the hallway, and his whole team appeared.

Huh, apparently he wasn't alone at all. I couldn't help but feel a jolt of envy and a little jealousy. I pushed that aside. Now was not the time or the place. We still had a mission to complete.

And now more than ever, I wanted this to be truly over.

CHAPTER 9
LUCAS

As soon as we skidded to a stop right outside the entrance to the concrete bunker built underground in the middle of nowhere, I dashed out of the vehicle.

The rest of the team hadn't bothered to try to stop me at this point. I'd already screwed up the plan by pulling up outside rather than a kilometre away. Urgency had me ignoring their grumbles.

The drive had taken too long, each second that passed burying me deeper and deeper into a spiral of claustrophobic despair.

In retrospect, the explosion had probably been unnecessary, but with no idea of who was in the bunker, I'd thought going in fast and hard was best. From Callen's complaints as I'd raced through the now-blown-open doorway, you'd have thought he'd never done anything as irresponsible before.

He absolutely had and far too many times for me to count.

I followed my nose. It led me to an open doorway. Once there, I all but stumbled in relief. Valeria was wedged under Ethan's broad body, both of them covered in concrete dust and a little debris.

I dragged in a breath, my chest expanding, muscles loosening. As Ethan looked my way, all wide-eyed and giving me crap, I glanced to their side, my growing smirk slipping off my lips.

Maya.

It was really her.

I felt the blood drain from my face, dread threatening to creep into the crevices of my mind.

After all this time, she was back from the dead and continuing to try to blow up my world.

She'd taken my child. Screwed with Ethan.

No.

I straightened, swallowing back the bile churning my gut. The woman had stolen too much from me already. This had to stop. No more.

"Dad?"

I jerked at Valeria's voice, the softness there taking me by surprise. Concern coloured her voice and gentled her expression as she took a step towards me. While hurt pulsed off her, she continued forwards until I swooped her in a hug, my limbs trembling as I held her tightly.

I breathed her in, my soul singing in gratitude that she was okay. She was here, alive, and holding me as firmly as I held her.

"I'm so sorry," I whispered against her ear, not controlling the shake or the sadness in my tone. "I have so much to tell you."

She nodded against my shoulder, a shaky whoosh of air leaving her, revealing her vulnerability.

"Are you okay?" Reluctantly, I held on to her arms and eased back to rake my gaze over her body. I'd already noted the redness of her neck, the puncture wounds, and the dried blood.

Making eye contact, she bobbed her head and stroked her fingers against her neck before dropping her hand. Almost instantly, the softness surrounding her slipped away. The woman before me morphing into the steadfast agent she was known to be both broke my heart and made me proud.

I dropped my hands, and she moved back a step, finally looking away and taking in the rest of the team. She nodded, quickly hiding the sliver of emotion that appeared for a tiny moment when her eyes landed briefly on Tarka.

A gentle thud drew my attention to Ethan. In ill-fitting clothes and covered in dust, he looked ridiculously sexy. Warmth pooled in my gut, our gazes connecting for a second time. He'd protected Valeria—even though she likely wouldn't have needed it. Still, he'd stepped up, done what I hadn't been able to do.

His lips tugged up just a little, his eyes telling me everything. He was okay. He was relieved.

My chest expanded, my fingers twitching, wanting to reach out to him. But I couldn't. There was too much unsaid and unknown. Plus, the audience around us was one thing, but my ex stirring awake was a step too far.

"It looks like we missed the party," Callen said, cutting through the tension as he stepped into the room, his shoulder brushing mine briefly before he nudged me lightly and flicked me a wink. Then he looked at Ethan. "Wilder, you're alive." He pushed out his bottom lip and nodded. "I'm impressed, man.

Ethan expelled a heavy breath. "What the fuck ever, man."

My lips twitched despite the shitshow that was still unravelling.

"You might want to get on top of this fucked-up situation before Hornell figures out what's going on here and disappears into the ether."

We all froze at Ethan's words, backs straightening as we went on high alert.

"Hornell's responsible for this?" I asked, running a cursory gaze over Maya. So far, her finger and shoulder had twitched. It wouldn't take much longer. I didn't want to see her eyes, hating that Valeria's were so similar.

"They were after Wilder here. Something about a chip." Valeria headed back to where we'd found them and picked up a laptop off the floor. She blew on it, turned it upside down, and shook it. "I think I was a little collateral and a lot compulsion."

My jaw ticked. Maya had been unhinged for over half of our relationship. All attempts to protect Valeria were well and truly burned to ash. It was beyond time that she knew the truth. I just wished I'd had the courage to share with her on my terms.

"Meaning what, exactly?" Callen asked.

"That I arrived at the old water station too early, and rather than race away with my buddy bear here" —Ethan huffed a quiet snort of laughter, but Valeria didn't break her stride—"she took one look at me and thought it would be a super awesome idea to try to play happy family and bring me to the dark side."

"You sure this kid isn't your secret love child with Kent? 'Cause I swear—Ow, fuck!" Michaels was cut off with a punch in the gut from Kent.

I dropped my head in exasperation and fondness. Rather than giving me shit and questioning why I never opened up to him, Michaels, like all my team, was rolling with this pretty huge development.

"The dark side being working for Hornell?"

Thank God Callen was somehow keeping things together.

"Oh God, please don't tell me she wants Hornell to be your new daddy or something."

And he went and blew it.

"For fuck's sake, Callen." Kent's exasperation was a replication of my own. "Valeria, I wish I could say I don't work with idiots"—she waved her hand at the evidence—"but clearly I can't plead my defence. Maya is about to wake up. Is there anything that needs discussing away from here, or is that pointless?"

Valeria offered Kent a genuine smile. Damn, I missed that look on her face. It had been so long since I'd seen her, let alone with such a genuine amused reaction.

"We may as well talk this out right here. I'm not sure we'll get anything from her but—"

Ethan cut in. "Maya's under Hornell's influence." All our attention turned to him, but his gaze was on me as he continued. "I don't think it's a chip, not the one I worked with, but there's been some modifications. I think chemically induced."

Dread bunched my muscles tight. "How do you know?"

"Take a look at her eyes when she's awake. Plus, I know vampires are strong, but she definitely has something helping her up her ability to kick arse. She has a grip like a vice, way stronger than it should be. I've never seen anything like it before."

"I have," Callen said.

We all had. The last couple of years had been hella busy with the amount of terrifying developments made in chemical and technical enhancement. All illegal for all the right reasons, considering how brutal and morally wrong the experimentation was.

My mind raced, trying to connect the dots.

"She was also wearing this earpiece." Valeria tugged a small device from her pocket. "We're hoping we can trace the feed."

"Do you mind?" Kent stepped forwards.

"Go for it." My daughter passed it to Kent, who immediately left the room with Smythe following her. If a trace was possible, the two of them would get it.

A grunt alerted us to Maya waking. A low moan followed, her leg shifting. The rattle of metal chains clicking echoed around the room. Immediately she froze, her eyes springing open.

Wide-eyed, she gazed at us, hesitating briefly on

Valeria before settling on me. A sneer contorted her features. My gut squeezed, my heart crawling into my throat.

How had she manipulated me so thoroughly? How had she managed to make me doubt and question my sanity, not to mention my own worth?

Hate poured off her, slamming into me with such ferocity that it threatened to buckle my knees. She'd worn the same expression three months after I'd discovered the truth about her identity, about why she'd married me, built a fake life with me, even had a child with me. It had bled into her features as she'd watched me being beaten and clawed at. As she'd stared on with sinister amusement and disgust that she'd had to waste so much time on me and my pathetic existence.

Her lips pulled back, revealing fangs and spittle, and then she was gone from my view. Broad shoulders, a bushy beard, and an intense gaze took her place.

My shoulders sagged as I took a breath, focussing intently on Ethan. Before me, he stood as an impenetrable wall, guarding me from the poison and the painful memories Maya was responsible for.

Without speaking, without explanation or instruction, he took hold of my arm and turned me slowly towards the doorway before he stepped in front of me and led me out. I kept my eyes on his back, not daring to look around or listen to the sharp, venomous words falling free from Maya.

I didn't want to see my team's expressions, their sympathy. Hell, maybe their disgust that their boss didn't have his shit together.

Taking one step in front of the other, I followed where Ethan led. He drew me out of the room and down the corridor before ushering me into an empty office. The door snicked shut, cutting off Maya's shouting in an instant.

Warm, strong arms clamped around me, holding me close and tight, reassuring and reminding me I was okay. I wasn't alone.

I hugged him back, squeezing him tight and inhaling his scent. Morning dew on pine needles. Absorbing his quiet strength, I took a breath, my muscles easing the longer we stayed this way.

"Why do I let her pull this reaction from me?" I eventually whispered. I couldn't hide away like this. If I did, it would be like she was winning. For years she'd taken my power. Losing any more to her meant I wouldn't be able to look at myself in the mirror, let alone step foot into work.

Ethan didn't release me as he spoke. "From the little I know, I imagine it was what she was trained to do. Add in her inclination for cruelty, and I don't think anyone would have a choice."

After everything had gone down, the SICB had insisted on mandatory therapy. I'd jumped into it willingly. Rationally, I understood what Ethan said was true. I was also fully aware of my coping mechanisms—some not exactly healthy—and my limits.

Maya was my limit, and I hated that was the case.

"I don't think I can be in the same room as her."

"Then you don't be in the same room as her." Ethan angled back, the understanding in his gaze almost drawing out more emotion than I was comfortable with, which was ludicrous considering the situation.

"But my team…. Valeria…. What will—"

"I'm sure Callen will insist that you *and* Valeria are not there. You're too close to all of this. Everything about Maya being here is personal."

I leaned forwards, seeking comfort by dropping my head and pressing it against his chest. When he dotted a kiss on the top, I melted a little more. I inhaled and tensed at the metallic scent, standing bolt upright and nearly smacking him in the chin in the process. "You're hurt?" I studied his face, taking in his tight smile. "Show me."

"I'm fine."

I arched my brow, fighting to not grind my

molars. This right here was the issue. My struggle, my seeking his support, didn't make me fragile or incompetent.

Without saying a word, he lifted the too-tight T-shirt, revealing his muscular chest and abs covered in a smattering of hair that I absolutely wanted to run my hands over.

"It's healing. It just hurts like a fucker."

The slash on his side was red and raw but looked to be recovering. They'd split some of the ink in his skin, damaging the design a little. I angled closer, scenting him, frustrated I hadn't realised before that he'd been injured. Singed skin, sickly and tainted, reached me. My brows shot high. "You were burnt?"

He had the grace to look guilty and lifted his sleeves to reveal the burns. I winced. Layers of skin had been damaged. It would take some time to heal.

Our gazes connected, and I readjusted my stance, more than aware he watched my every move. "If you're injured, you tell me. If you're in pain, you're not a prick who suffers in silence."

Amusement that I wanted to kiss off his face appeared, and he crossed his arms. "Since when did you become the boss of me?"

"Since you were working on my team after fucking up."

He snorted. "Don't hold back, Matt. Tell me how you really feel."

A shudder rippled down my spine at the sound of my name on his lips.

"I'm sure this might come as a surprise, but it's been a long time since I've had a boss. I'm not sure I play too well with one."

His teasing mixed oh so perfectly with his smartarse mouth.

"I don't know. I think you handled your boss pretty darn well on the kitchen table." Heat hit my cheeks, and I clamped my lips together, barely believing those words had spilled from me.

It didn't mean I regretted them. Rather I was surprised as hell that I found it in me to flirt and tease.

Ethan's eyes darkened, and he took a step closer, his voice dropping to a husky whisper. "Oh, I handled you well, did I? Might need to test that theory again."

My breath hitched as the heat between us intensified. "Maybe you should. Just to be sure."

His smirk grew, wicked and promising. "Don't tempt me, Matt. I'm not one to back down from a challenge."

Before I could respond, Ethan closed the distance between us, his mouth capturing mine in a searing kiss. It was possessive and hungry, filled with a promise that made my knees weak. I clung to him, desperate to feel more, to get lost in the sensation.

A throat clearing at the door pulled us apart. Shaw stood there, looking super embarrassed and awkward, but there was a glint of amusement in his eyes. "Uh, sorry to interrupt, but we need you both."

Ethan's hand lingered on my waist as he turned to Shaw. "We'll be right there."

Shaw nodded, his eyes darting between us. "Right. Just… uhm, is this something I need to keep my mouth shut about?"

I choked down an awkward laugh before sighing and shaking my head. "Shaw, get out of here."

Hell, the whole damn unit would know in less than five seconds. Not a chance he wouldn't be telling his boyfriend or his best friend.

Shaw nodded quickly and backed away. As he left, Ethan leaned in close, his breath warm against my ear. "This isn't over."

I shivered, anticipation curling in my stomach. "I'm counting on it."

It felt right, even in the middle of my world cracking apart, with all the lies and my fears rippling to the surface.

As we left, I had a decision to make: could I face Maya? Did I even want to?

I had just a few seconds to figure that out as we walked down the corridor, the flickering lights guiding our way. As we edged closer, Ethan's palm found mine. I glanced at our joined hands.

I was strong and capable. I was also a mess, and I definitely didn't have a life outside of work. Nor did I have a relationship with my daughter.

But all the latter could change. It felt like it had already started to.

What was it about the man at my side, someone I barely knew, who seemed to simply understand me and my needs and what made me tick?

"Have you decided?"

I shot him a look. It was foolish at this point to be surprised by his ability to read me.

"I want to go in, but I'll let Callen take the lead."

"Okay." With a final squeeze of my hand, he released me, and we followed the voices and stepped back into the room where Maya remained chained up.

"Huh." I darted my gaze around, wondering who was responsible.

Michaels stood there with a syringe and didn't look the least bit sorry. He shrugged. "She was talking shit and wasn't being helpful. Plus she was giving me a damn headache."

My "Fair" appeared to catch him by surprise as Michaels burst out in shocked laughter.

"Shit, if getting laid was all it took for you to—" An elbow to the gut from Shaw cut him off. "*Oof*, for fuck's sake. What?" Michaels looked genuinely perplexed while I balanced on a fine edge between mortification and amusement. "He seems more chilled. Plus Wilder can't be such a fuckface if bossman likes him."

My daughter snorted.

Immediately, Michaels's eyes grew to the size of full moons as he faced Valeria. "Shit, that's the last thing you want to hear or think about. But to be fair, we've only sort of heard about his attempt to date another evil bitch."

I wanted the ground to open up and swallow me whole.

"So after finding out bossman had a wife, let alone a daughter, we're kinda rooting that a guy will do the job of not screwing him over." Michaels stared pointedly at Ethan, who wore an expression of passive indifference. That didn't mean I couldn't spot the glee in his eyes.

Arsehole.

"I have no issues ending you," Michaels carried on, apparently on a roll. "You might be a big motherfucker, but screw with Lucas and you'll be dead. You won't see me coming."

At his side, Shaw palmed his face, refusing to look at the gigantic hole his boyfriend was digging. Tarka, another arsehole, chuckled, eyes wide and thoroughly enjoying himself. Valeria was eating this up, momentarily cutting through all the hurt that existed between us and loving my embarrassment.

"Michaels, unless you want me to destroy you and make sure you're assigned the shittiest jobs imaginable for the rest of your sorry existence, shut the fuck up," Kent hollered from outside the room.

I dropped my head and shook it. Kent deserved a pay rise. Thank goodness she was my second and apparently could command the team better than I could.

Callen, for maybe the third time in his existence, brought us back on track rather than encouraging my team, saying, "I cannot believe I'm the grown-up again with you guys. This is so fucked up." He glanced around the unit and rolled his eyes.

I'd need to tell Thatch about how he stepped up. He wouldn't believe it, though.

"Lucas," he started, and our gazes connected. "We need to move out and head to a secure location. Are you good to travel with Smythe and Kent and work on the way? We need to get that trace. Stat."

"Yeah, of course."

He glanced at Ethan. "Wilder, do you need medical attention? We'll send Michaels with you for protection detail if you do."

"No."

Callen's brows jumped high while I bit down on my lip at Ethan's gruffness.

With a sigh, Callen asked, "Have you at least stopped bleeding?"

"Yes."

I cut in. "He's healing okay. His burns will take longer than the laceration on his side, but he's not going to bleed out."

Seemingly satisfied, Callen gave me an up-nod and turned to Tarka. "Do you have somewhere to be, or are you in this?"

His lips lifting into a smile, Tarka threw me a wink before answering Callen. "My team will support you. Whatever you need. We have a secure location close by that you're free to use."

Turning to me, Callen raised his brow, silently asking for my opinion.

"Yeah, makes sense. There's still too much unknown."

"Maya somehow knew about my safe house outside of Warwick. She had eyes or ears on the place."

My attention snapped to Ethan. She did?

I willed heat from touching my cheeks, dreading to think exactly what she said to Ethan for him to know that.

He shrugged, a "couldn't care less" expression forming. But those damn eyes of his spoke of heat and promise as he refused to look away.

Seriously, how he managed to do that while appearing like he didn't have a care in the world was ridiculously impressive.

Either completely unaware or ignoring the way Ethan was eye fucking me, Callen said, "Okay. In that case, Tarka, we'd appreciate the assist. If we get more details en route, we'll make a decision, depending on the location. We're not a hundred percent sure it was Hornell at the end of the earpiece."

The news was disappointing.

He continued, "Even if it wasn't, Maya was definitely taking orders, though, so we're hopeful." He glanced around the room, saying, "Let's move out."

We did so, Michaels and Shaw gathering an unconscious Maya while the rest of us headed to the vehicles.

As soon as I was settled, I accepted the laptop from Kent.

"Thanks."

She nodded.

"I'll complete a report and get a crew out here." I went through all the procedures I needed to follow, making sure to complete the necessary logs and files. While the priority was the trace, unease stirred in my gut until I managed to get everything squared away.

We'd already gone above Durrant's head on this trip, so at least by ensuring all the paperwork was completed and those who needed the intel would be notified, I was able to breathe easier.

Valeria drove, having surprised me by saying she wanted to be in the same vehicle with me. Ethan had hesitated when she'd staked her claim, and for a moment, I'd thought he might argue, but after a beat and an intense stare where I was sure he could read my mind, he'd nodded and got into a vehicle with Hart without a word.

"What have you shared with the SICB?" Valeria asked when I finally saved the last report.

I glanced to my side, taking in her profile, which was a study in contrasts—an elegant blend of inherited traits that marked her as unique. Her skin, pale as moonlight and a testament to our vampire heritage, gave her an ethereal glow. Her eyes, a legacy from her mother, were striking and deep, with the unmistakable almond shape and dark hue of her half-Korean ancestry. They held an intensity and intelligence that revealed her years, always calculating, always assessing.

Her nose, straight and refined, was a feature reminiscent of my grandmother's, giving her a grace that contrasted beautifully with her sharp-edged persona as a seasoned agent. Though, technically, I had no idea who she was currently working for.

As I watched her, I couldn't help but feel a swell of pride. She was more than just my daughter; she was a formidable ally and a brilliant mind. Her presence was a reminder of the good that could come from even the darkest of legacies.

When she cleared her throat, I answered quickly, "I've not reached out directly to Durrant. Neither has Callen." Not keeping Durrant in the loop went against the grain, and if I thought too hard about it, it was likely I'd do something foolish like read her in.

Not that I didn't trust her. That was absolutely not the issue.

Callen and I had agreed that the fewer people we brought in, the safer the operation and the less likely Hornell would get wind of us. Even the reports I'd filled in were on a timer—not set to go to the relevant logs for another eight hours.

Leaving bodies in the bunker was far from ideal, but the team had taken photographs and found a freezer they'd moved them to. Callen's suggestion that we'd get an A-plus for effort would absolutely not be the way this went down, but we'd done it anyway. Kent had also managed to capture the front door surveillance to get the details of the guards who were injured and had escaped.

We'd catch up with them when all of this was over.

"That doesn't sound like something you'd usually do," Valeria observed. There wasn't a challenge in her tone, more like curiosity. "Is this the bear being a bad influence or Callen?" This time teasing entered her voice.

I chuckled, grasping on to the olive branch. When was the last time we'd done this—been comfortable enough with each other to tease and smile?

"This is my decision as well as my division leader's."

Kent's snort drew my attention. "Don't let him fool you, Valeria. Your dad's been known to bypass protocol a time or two over the years."

I rolled my eyes good-naturedly at Kent, though I didn't deny her words. While I'd only led the ITU for a couple of years, Kent and I went way back—unfortunately, courtesy of her sister whom Michaels had previously mentioned.

That wasn't anything I needed to open up about

to my daughter with my team witnessing the exchange.

Valeria side-eyed me. Her subsequent "You seem happier, more relaxed" meant she wasn't as concerned with getting up close and personal in front of an audience.

Not wanting to shut her down—I'd take any conversation I could get—I answered honestly, "There's a lot I need to share with you about Maya and her behaviour." I actively avoided looking at her. "Maya's ability to do her job would have been impressive if she wasn't so dangerous or toxic."

"A brutal combination of gaslighting and torture must be hard to break free from."

Surprise jolted me into sitting up straighter. How—

"You weren't as great as you thought you were at keeping secrets or me in the dark growing up."

My heart stuttered.

"And I'm not saying that to make you feel guilty. If anything, I'm furious at myself for knowing something was off, almost wrong, but I was so damn stubborn that I couldn't see it. When you intervened with that case in North Korea...." She shook her head and exhaled while I winced. "I thought you were the one who was too controlling, but that wasn't the case, was it?"

When she caught my eye, I shook my head despite saying, "I was trying to protect you, so I suppose there was an element of taking control away from you. But I didn't want you anywhere near North Korea. By that point, I thought Maya had died."

"Not in London?"

"No." I let her see my guilt, my regret. "In Darwin. We had her on the run for a while. It took us months to finally locate her. Obviously, she didn't die in an explosion a joint task force orchestrated like we'd thought. And while I don't know where she's been or what she's been responsible for since then, from what we've learned today, it's not been anything good."

Valeria nodded as she switched the headlights on. The day was quickly turning to night as we continued to travel towards the outskirts of Melbourne. The road ahead was a dark ribbon winding through undulating hills. As we sped onwards, the dimming light cast long, stretching shadows over the landscape.

The road was mostly empty, save for the occasional pair of headlights piercing through the darkness in the opposite direction. Pockets of mist began to form in the low-lying areas, creeping across the fields and onto the road like ghostly fingers.

Valeria's focus was intense, her hands gripping the steering wheel as she manoeuvred the car through the gently winding road. The rhythmic thrum of the tyres on asphalt was the only sound, punctuated occasionally by the distant cry of a night bird or the rustle of unseen creatures in the under-brush, only audible because of our enhanced hearing.

The truth about Darwin, about Maya, dredged up memories both recent and raw. The pursuit had been relentless and exhausting—months spent chasing shadows and whispers, always a step behind. Hell if it didn't give me a sense of déjà vu, reminding me so much of everything we'd been through chasing down Hornell.

But now, finally, after all this time, we had her in custody.

Maybe this would give me the chance to finally let go of the past and move on.

The headlights cut through the growing darkness, illuminating the way ahead, the gentle tapping of Kent and Smythe on their laptops accompanying the hum of the electric engine and reminding me they'd heard everything.

That was okay. Secrets were wearing.

I opened up my laptop, knowing I should get back to work and support Kent and Smythe. As I opened the lid, movement ahead in the darkness caught my attention. I leaned forwards, needing to squint despite my ability to see well even in the depths of night.

"What the—" I started. "Move. Move. Move." I grabbed at the steering wheel, tugging a hard right.

Valeria responded immediately, and I just hoped like hell the others in our convoy did the same.

Bright lights pierced the air, nothing like the headlights we'd been seeing sporadically over the past twenty minutes. An explosion sounded five metres to our right, shaking the SUV as Valeria navigated off-road.

Voice tight but controlled, she gritted out, "What's the plan here?"

"Kent, what do you see?" I asked, confident she'd already be on it as I tapped on my ear, connecting to the unit's comms. I heard the beep from the others' earpieces asking them to connect.

Callen's voice filled my ear. "What have we got?"

"One more second," Kent responded.

Valeria turned again, the headlights of the convoy following us getting some distance between the vehicles that had been coming towards us and the shots they'd sent our way.

"Holy shit." Kent stared at me. "It's Hornell. He's on site."

I did a double-take out of the window, staring into the darkness. "How sure are you?"

"Pretty fucking sure, since he's looking directly up at the lens in the drone."

I'd never been more grateful for Kent and her foresight, which had prompted her to launch a drone to fly overhead when we'd first left the airstrip.

"Dad?"

"Callen?"

"Safeties off," he ordered, and I swore I heard glee in his voice.

Looked like we were going on the attack. "Reverse ambush?" I clarified, remembering a similar mission with Callen when we'd both been field agents a few years back.

"You know it." There was that glee again.

Tarka's amused voice came through comms. "Is someone going to fill us in?" Not that I was surprised he was getting a rush with being chased down by eight—I glanced behind me, counting—no, *nine* vehicles in pursuit.

He'd always loved this high-octane drama.

Me, not so much. I glanced quickly at Valeria. Her eyes were bright as she cast me a glance, a grin on her face.

Hell. I shook my head and snorted as Callen explained over comms the plan to put some distance between us and the cars pursuing us, which would give us the chance to spin and settle in a line so we could take the fight to them.

"I always wanted to go into battle with you at least once, Dad."

I narrowed my gaze, not sure if she was teasing or not. "Is that right?" My voice was strained as she floored it, following Callen's instructions.

"Hell yes. Me and you kicking arse—"

"… and forgetting to take names is the saying in the ITU," Callen supplied helpfully.

"But yeah, we've got this, Dad."

She squeezed my hand, and my heart expanded with love.

"Five seconds," Callen warned.

I took out one of my guns, switched off the safety, and latched on to the buckle of the seat belt, ready to release and get into position.

"Three… two… one. Now!"

The cars split apart, turned, and slammed to a stop beside one another, headlights off but ready to be trained on the approaching vehicles. The echo of belts unlatching and doors opening followed. Then we were out, taking position behind the open doors, listening to the engines closing in, the fast rumble of tyres over the bumpy terrain.

I glanced to my right, gaze connecting with

Ethan's two vehicles over. A brief nod my way and he raised his gun, getting into position.

I relaxed my shoulders, doing the same thing.

It was time to end this.

"Now," Callen ordered.

On cue, all our cars' lights switched on, the main beams lighting up the soil and dirt and the cars racing our way. Two slowed while the others charged forwards.

We waited, breaths held until the vehicles were almost upon us. Then we unleashed a torrent of gunfire.

The front cars buckled under the assault, tyres blowing out, metal crumpling as they skidded to a stop. The occupants were forced out, shouting and scrambling for cover. I took aim, my gun steady as I picked off targets methodically. Glass shattered, bullets whizzed past, and the air was thick with the scent of gunpowder and blood.

The night erupted in chaos as gunfire tore through the air, all violence and desperation. Bullets zinged past, smashing windshields and puncturing rubber, sending the enemy vehicles skidding out of control. Sparks flew as metal clashed with metal, the screeches blending with the shouts of our pursuers. One car, its front tyre blown out, veered off course, flipping and rolling in a cacophony of crunching metal and shattering glass.

I took aim, my trigger finger steady and relentless. Three bodies dropped from the enemy convoy. I grunted, jerking as my shoulder burned from a grazing bullet. I ignored the pain, focussing on searching for Hornell.

Glass rained down as windows shattered, glittering shards glinting in the harsh headlights. I ducked, firing back while scanning the scene for Hornell, the man responsible for so much misery.

A grenade arced through the air and landed with a heavy thud behind our line of defence. "Grenade!" Shaw shouted. We scattered, diving for cover as the explosion rocked the ground, sending one of our cars flipping end over end before crashing in a fiery heap.

I didn't remain on the hard ground for long. With a wheeze and ringing ears, I pushed myself up, spotting the onslaught of Hornell's modified guards. Hand-to-hand combat it was.

I bared my fangs, my instincts taking over as I tore through flesh, my strength and speed overwhelming the shifters who fought back fiercely.

The irony wasn't lost on me as I fought to stop the bloodshed while tearing out a lion's throat.

Desperation fuelled my every move. My focus

was split between the battle and the search for Valeria and Ethan. I spotted Ethan, still in human form, grappling with a woman who slashed at his chest with a knife. I couldn't look away, knowing I was too far to help, but I tried. Tried to get to him. To move.

Kent moved faster, a shot ringing out as she took the woman down. I nodded in relief, but out of the corner of my eye, I saw something that made my blood run cold.

Hornell. He stood there with Maya awake and uncuffed beside him, but it was the sight of my daughter with a gun to her head that froze me in my tracks. My heart pounded, fear and rage a powerful combination that threatened to buckle my knees.

"No."

In the chaos, I kept my eyes on Hornell, rage burning within me. He held my daughter, a shield, his eyes locked on mine with a cold, calculating smile. My heart pounded as I sought a way to end this nightmare, save my daughter, and finally bring Hornell to justice.

CHAPTER 10

WILDER

One second, I was following Matt's gaze, my stomach dropping as I turned towards where Valeria stood, her chin squared and defiance in her eyes while a gun was held to her temple, and the next, it was like a vacuum sucked the air from the open space of blood and carnage.

My reaction snowballed.

Kent, who'd saved my arse, froze, her grip on her gun tightening. Michaels, who was to my right, enacted a similar pattern.

Thank fuck Hornell's minions seemed to do the same—relaxing their stances at some silent order.

Matt was frozen, his body deathly still, the guns in his hands hanging limply at his sides.

"It's amazing the power someone can wield when they have the means and the foresight."

My nostrils twitched, the side of my lips struggling not to lift into a snarl. I'd only seen old photographs of the man before me, taken when he'd been a captain. What none of them had captured was the cruelty in his gaze, nor had they conveyed the instability.

"Now that I have your attention, why don't you all take a moment to hand your weapons to my team." Hornell flicked his gaze from Matt to me before settling on one of the women in his detail.

As one, his team approached us. Each step they took sent throbs of tension through every cell in my body. I cast a look at Callen, watching his reaction. With Matt's back to me, I had no way of knowing what the play was here.

Someone reached Callen first; he stood there, not moving, not speaking. A miracle, perhaps, since he wasn't known for keeping his mouth shut. What he didn't do was hand over his gun.

Hornell, watching the exchange, tilted his head slightly. Another woman, a bear shifter, approached Matt, stopping when she stood before him with her palm outstretched.

Goose bumps broke free on my skin, my muscles tensing, ready to move, ready to rain down hell.

All it took was a slash of Maya's knife down Valeria's cheek, and Matt's shoulders sagged as he released his hold on the gun, relinquishing it into the bear's hand.

Fuck. It couldn't end like this.

Valeria didn't flinch or cower, her ramrod straight back along with her sneer making it clear how pissed off she was.

Yet still, none of us spoke.

I didn't "speak" SICB, not having any clue what the team would be thinking, would be planning. In my old unit, the team on the ground had protocols for this. Frustration bubbled through me. I should have asked. Hell, I should have been told.

When both the ITU and Tarka's security team handed over their weapons, I had no choice but to give up my two guns. As one of Hornell's shifters patted me down, I growled, unable to rein in the snarl.

Hornell tutted, a wide grin appearing and aimed at me. "Here's what's going to happen," he said, his finger resting on the trigger.

I straightened up, dropping my growl, holding back a victorious shiver of awareness when the shifter stepped away from me, having not found the two blades I'd squirreled away in my back pockets.

"Wilder will come with me and hand over the schematics that I previously asked for so politely."

I assumed "polite" was synonymous with "red-hot poker."

"At this stage in this tiresome cat-and-mouse game we're playing, honestly, I expected better from all of you. So it ends here. Wilder, you will come with me. In exchange, *Vance* will—"

Two things happened simultaneously. A hole appeared on Hornell's forehead and a knife landed in Maya's chest.

Then carnage.

I grabbed my blades and launched both into the shifter's neck who'd patted me down. He dropped immediately as a barrage of shots, groans, and splatters of blood from flying daggers rent the air.

Ringing deafened me, my adrenaline on overtime as I picked up my guns and spun, searching for another target. Heavy pants tore out of me, my eyes widening as I saw our team upright, on high alert as they studied the terrain, dead bodies at our feet.

"There were a couple of vehicles that broke away earlier. Check if they're around," Tarka ordered.

Three members of his unit broke free, their guns back in their hands, their expressions fierce.

I followed their movements, not quite trusting

what had happened. I hadn't even seen who'd made the shot or hit their mark.

Callen said, "Seriously, how fucking hard is it to get someone's name right? Piece of shit." He shook his head in disgust and stowed away his gun.

Apparently, the threat was over, and I suspected Callen hit the bull's-eye with his shot to Hornell's head.

Then who—

Matt was moving, racing towards his daughter, then tugging her into a fierce hug. He palmed the back of her head as she held on tightly while he whispered something I deliberately refrained from listening in on. I stood back, my chest tight, struggling to process everything.

I hadn't taken a life in years. And that had only been once. As a cyber security specialist, it didn't exactly call for death and mayhem. Blood, still wet on my hands, felt uncomfortable. A least earlier when it had been encrusted in my beard, I hadn't been able to see the mess I was in. I needed a shower and to process and to hold on to Matt and lose myself in his heat and his kisses and his—

I swallowed hard. That wasn't the plan. I'd promised to be on the next plane out of here when all of this was over.

Wiping my hands on my borrowed jeans, I looked

up when Matt's movement caught my attention. He released Valeria and bent down towards Maya's still form. My eyes widened when he tugged free the knife, wiped it clean on his black pants, and pocketed it in a small sheath on his belt.

Holy fuck.

That shouldn't be hot, only because the whole killing someone definitely shouldn't be sexy. But from the flutter in my chest and the inappropriate thickening of my cock, it didn't seem like I'd got the memo.

His gaze snapped up, landing on mine, ensnaring me.

My breath whooshed out. Need. Desire. Confusion. Each emotion I was sure I saw in the depth of his piercing gaze could have been my own.

"Callen, make the call to Durrant." The cool order spilled out of Matt with clear, practiced ease. "Kent, get your drone overhead and help check for stragglers, then get this mess recorded."

Reminded, with undeniable certainty, that Matt was absolutely Team Leader Agent Lucas in this moment, I stared on, marvelling at the change before me. This was undoubtedly the man I'd first met, giving out concise orders, asking for things from his team, who wouldn't hesitate to follow his requests. Even Callen.

He continued dishing out instructions. At some point he'd found a first-aid kit, and he was now wiping a disinfectant pad over Valeria's face. While disgruntled and, I suspected, a little embarrassed at the attention, she seemed to take his care in good stride, only rolling her eyes a little.

Then there was me, standing here like a fish out of water with no clear direction and feeling out of my depth. I wasn't part of this team, didn't have a leader, a direction.

I edged away towards one of the vehicles, an uncomfortable ache in my chest. As I walked, the two units around me worked with loud, chatty precision. The jokes were perhaps macabre considering the destruction and death, but I understood it—their relief that this was over, their joy that they were alive and had survived the confrontation relatively unscathed.

When I reached one of the vehicles with the boot open, I grabbed for a small first-aid kit. Blood oozed out of slashes on my arms and chest. I needed to get cleaned up and hold a couple of the wounds together to help speed up healing. Then... I hesitated. I glanced around me. Nobody paid a lick of attention as they supported one another, cleaned up. A few were on tablets, others on important phone calls—at least, I assumed so from their serious expressions.

I needed to get the fuck out of here and on a plane. The uncomfortable twist of loneliness, the reminder that I was an outsider shone a spotlight on the hollowness in my gut.

Fuck that.

I'd made peace with my solitary existence a long time ago. Was it the reason why I could be such a cunt and pushed people away? Abso-fucking-lutely.

With a wince, I peeled away the sweat- and bloodstained T-shirt that was in ruins. Two of the three slashes would just need a clean. The third…. I scrunched my nose. It would need stitches or at least glue. The deep one was nestled in the mat of hair on my pec, which meant I needed to shave the damn thing to get access unless I wanted my hair to be glued or stitched down.

Just bloody peachy.

I tore open a packet of alcohol wipes and swiped at one of the smaller cuts, scrunching my nose at the sting. The sheet coloured quickly, capturing more blood from my hands than off my body.

I shook my head. Maybe I should just wait till I was at the airport. Though there wasn't a chance I'd be let in the building in the state I was in.

"Fuck," I grumbled, throwing the soiled sheet in a paper bag in the back of the SUV.

"You need some help there?"

I turned. Valeria stood a few metres from me, a wry smile aimed in my direction.

Forming a tight smile, I shook my head. "I've got it." I glanced away, picking up another wipe and continuing to swipe the blood. My muscles rippled at the stinging, and I gritted my teeth, having to scrub harder at some of the more-difficult-to-remove stains.

"Bloody hell." The wipe was pulled from my grip and thrown in the car before Valeria gathered another, saying, "You're so damn stubborn. That I know that despite not even knowing you should have you worried."

"That right?" I aimed for disinterested.

"Uh-huh." She examined the deeper cut on my chest, prodding lightly around the edge.

"Ouch, fuck. Careful."

She pulled away and rolled her eyes. "That's going to need stitches."

"No shit," I groused. Brushing her hand away, I grabbed a bundle of gauze and pressed it against the deeper cut that still trickled blood. "I just need some wound-closure strips for now."

Before I could reach into the kit, Valeria was there, rooting around. I took a good, long look at her, trying to get a read on how she was handling everything.

"I'm fine." There was a pinch to her tone that had

me immediately holding up my hands in self-defence.

"I didn't say a word."

"You didn't need to. Like I told Dad, I'm fine… for now, which means I'm dealing and coping the best I can and focussing on getting shit done. Whatever comes after when I process properly, I'll figure out then."

I shut down the sympathy trying to tug my eyebrows low. I suspected she wouldn't take too kindly to that.

"What's your plan?" she asked, changing the subject and holding the strips in her hand.

I frowned. "What do you mean?"

Our gazes connected before she pushed away my hand to focus on my injury.

"Well, you're here by yourself, avoiding the teams."

I was sure what she really thought was *"avoiding my dad,"* which, shit, I was doing. I shrugged, causing her to sigh as my chest moved in the process. "They're not my teams," I said bluntly. "I don't belong here."

She paused a second after pressing a second strip to my wound and made eye contact with me before shaking her head and placing a third.

"Did you ever consider that none of these guys felt like they belonged at some point?"

My brow furrowed, not wanting to think deeper about her words. "The plan has always been to catch the next flight out of here."

"You've got someone waiting for you at home?" She flicked her gaze up, her eyebrow arched high in challenge.

"Not like that, no." I clamped my lips shut. *Like that?* Why I'd said those words, as if she was searching for info about my relationship status, boggled my brain.

"I see." Another two strips and she stood, examining her work. "So, what is waiting for you, then?" Valeria tilted her head, her gaze assessing.

I stared back, refusing to answer.

She didn't need to know I lived in an apartment by myself. That I didn't know my neighbours, and beyond going to the gym that was two buildings away four times a week, it was rare I left my home.

My mum died when I was young. My dad, I hadn't known. There were no siblings that I knew about.

And after the cyber unit discredited me, it became crystal clear who my friends were. A grand tally of zero. The jury was still out about Hart, and when all that shit blew up, it was before I'd properly known him. I lived an existence that was best to not be examined too closely.

"I'll take over here."

My skin prickled and I jumped. Talk about embarrassing.

Valeria nodded as she passed by Matt, handing him a pack of alcohol wipes.

Heat touched my skin, the goose bumps refusing to disappear as he edged closer, and as he brushed by me, his shoulder touching my arm, I shivered, unable to hold back my reaction.

He didn't speak as he scanned my body with an assessing gaze. His brows shot up, though, when they settled on the open waist of the borrowed jeans, my thick trail visible.

"Jesus, Ethan." A groan followed, and his eyes snapped to mine. "This is what you were wearing the whole time?" Light pink travelled up his neck, hitting his cheeks. "How did I not see this earlier?" Heat filled his eyes, and I shifted uncomfortably under his scrutiny. A thick cock in these pants wouldn't leave anything to the imagination.

"I shifted at the bunker before I had the chance to strip." Gravel turned my voice raspy.

He swallowed hard, his eyes once again roaming my body, his fingers twitching, seeming like he wanted to follow the path of his gaze. If he did, I wouldn't have minded one bit, but I didn't think he'd be comfortable if my need for him overtook reason.

"Callen, Shaw, and Michaels are staying here to wait for Durrant and a team to arrive. The rest of us are catching a lift on Tarka's jet back to Sydney."

My heart hammered in my chest. So this was goodbye?

"Okay." I shuttered my expression and locked up any semblance of emotion that may sneak past my defences. "I'll grab a lift to the airport or maybe a hotel close by so I can wash up first."

Fuck, my passport, my gear. I closed my eyes, realizing everything was back in Brisbane. A second later, my eyes sprang wide open. "Shit, there was a fire." I didn't think I'd imagined that. After the explosion, everything was a little blurry. "My bag...." I trailed off.

I would need to organise a fake passport. I could reach out to George, who'd previously helped me when I was in Warwick.

"I have your bag."

My attention snapped to him, relief rushing into my chest thick and fast. "You do?"

He nodded, his intense gaze searching mine. "Your bag was left in the SUV we'd picked up."

A heavy whoosh of air escaped me. "That's great,

thanks." A relieved smile tilted my lips a fraction. "I'll grab that first."

"Before what?"

My smile slipped as reality set in. I had to go. "Before getting out of your hair and getting on the first flight to London."

When his lips tightened and formed a straight line, I held my breath, refusing to fidget under his scrutiny.

"Lucas." Callen calling his name broke our connection.

Matt glanced over his shoulder to where Callen stood with a phone to his ear and a tired expression. Hell, we all looked bolloxed. Covered in soot and blood, we were worse for wear. I definitely wouldn't be walking through the airport like this.

When Callen beckoned Matt over, he nodded before sparing me a glance and an up-nod. A second later, he turned on his heels and left.

That really was that, then.

The disappointment pressing against me threatened to smother my breath. I hated it. Detested the sensation of regret, of feeling let down. But each of those emotions were on me. I was responsible.

To be so invested in a man who I barely knew was beyond ridiculous. Sure, we'd shared some moments that had wedged themselves under my skin, but whatever this thing was between us could easily be blamed on our forced proximity and high-stress situations.

Fuck, I was a dick.

Squaring my shoulders, I rifled through one of the bags in the back of the SUV, looking for a tee of some sort. Coming up short, I searched a second, pausing when my hand touched fabric. A black T-shirt. I held it in front of me. Another snug fit, but it'd do.

I tugged it on, turning at the friendly chuckle.

Tarka eyed the shirt I'd commandeered that sported his firm's logo and name, Eclipse Security. "A tight fit, but it could work."

I snorted out a huff, not feeling any real amusement.

"I'm serious. We can order those in XXL, make it more comfortable."

My brows shot high, my reaction plain as day for him to see. Was he saying…? "Are you offering me a job?"

His one-armed shrug was anything but casual as he studied me. "Maybe. Are you looking?"

Taken aback by this whole conversation, my brain struggled to process his words. His "sort of" offer. After a beat, I landed on "I don't work well with others."

His laugh caught me by surprise. Loud and

booming, it pierced the air, turning more than a few heads our way. "I never took you for a bullshitter." He narrowed his gaze despite the smirk still being evident. "Sarcastic and a grumbly arsehole, sure. But someone who'd tell a bold-faced lie...."

I bristled, my muscles bunching as I turned to face him. "The fuck?"

A carefree lift of his shoulder preceded his "Just calling it as I see it."

"The hell is that supposed to mean?"

"You, today, and from what I've heard, the moment you stepped into Australia, have absolutely been a team player. The way you handled the situation, protected Vally, kicked some serious arse a few metres from where we stand—"

I shook my head, cutting him off. "I don't fight unless I have to. Give me a computer and I can get shit do—"

"Deal."

What the hell? "That's not what I—"

"I can give you the best equipment you can dream of having as well as the support. I can also pay you a shit-ton of money."

I took a good look at the man before me. He seemed genuine. I also knew he was close to Matt.

Matt.

If I took a position here, what would that mean for us? Did I have the guts to pursue something?

My chest constricted. Fuck, I wanted that. Desperately. Wanted to see if there was something real between us. Wanted to care for him, look out for him, spend hours worshipping his body as we took the time to learn everything there was to know about each other.

I cast my gaze away, searching for him. Immediately finding him still talking to Callen, I took a shallow breath. Would he want this?

As if sensing my attention, Matt angled towards me, our eyes connecting.

He didn't smile. He didn't wink. He didn't rush towards me, begging me not to leave. But there was something just out of reach. Something telling me that doing this could work.

Maybe some things were stronger than fate after all.

Maybe the lonely existence I'd accepted as my future wasn't set in stone.

"If I can be located to Sydney," I said, looking at Tarka, "I'm interested. Tell me more on the ride to the airstrip."

A satisfied smile and a pat on my arm and Tarka chuckled. "That's definitely a deal. Let's get this shit-show on the road."

WITH THE DIGITAL PEN POISED OVER THE SCREEN, I TOOK a deep breath. Fuck it. I signed the contract with zero flourish and gave the tablet back to Tarka. I had to hand it to the man, he was efficient.

We were close to the airstrip. The two of us sat in the back seat of the SUV while Prue, a member of his team, was at the wheel. In the time it took to leave the scene and get this far, he'd talked me through the position—mission tech support and all the finer details that it entailed—offered me a salary package I'd struggled not to gawk at and organised a contract.

"Do you want to head to the UK to pack up or…?" He trailed off, looking satisfied as he countersigned the contract.

"No." I shook my head. "There's a company I can use to do that for me and get my things sent over." If I left, I might wake up and realise I was making a huge mistake and putting a hell of a lot of pressure on a relationship that may never pan out.

But I wasn't only doing it for that.

It was time I wanted more. Building friendships and trust, having people at my back who I could count on—I wanted that. If I didn't, I wouldn't have flown halfway across the world in the first place. I'd done so out of guilt, sure, but also, the friendship I had with Hart was tentative at best. I hadn't wanted to lose it completely.

Hell, since I'd left Sydney, I'd barely talked to the man. There was a lot I had to make up for when it came to earning his trust. I hoped this past week was a strong start to that.

"No worries." Tarka tugged out a phone from a bag at his feet and passed it to me. "This is fully secure and now yours." He focussed back on his tablet. "I've just sent you the details for your new digs. It's about fifteen minutes—if traffic isn't a bastard—from headquarters. We have other hubs in each of the major cities around Australia, but Sydney is our home base." His smile turned sly, eyes filling with amusement when he added, "Just ten minutes in the other direction is a certain unit leader's pad too."

Despite my heating cheeks at being called out, I refused to look away as I narrowed my gaze. My pining clearly had not been as subtle as I'd thought. Though another dead giveaway was probably how I'd manhandled Matt at the bunker, then been caught with my tongue down his throat.

"Fuck off," I grunted. Boss or not, the man would need to get used to me.

Amused, Tarka chuckled and bobbed his head as the SUV pulled to a stop outside the hangar. "I think you're going to fit right in, Wilder." With that, he exited the car, and I lumbered out, searching for the sign to the washroom he'd told me about.

Most of us would need a washdown, so I had to make quick work of cleaning up and shaving around my wound to free up the space.

Spotting the sign, I headed first to the lockers. Here I would find fresh clothes. Just like Tarka told me, the locker was crammed full. I peered down at my still-bare feet, dreading the amount of scrubbing that I'd need to do to get the dirt trapped in small cuts from scraping rocks. In a third locker, I found a pair of boots, relieved men's shoe sizes worked the same way here as in the UK. I was in no fit state to figure out maths.

New clothes in hand, I headed into the small washroom. A shower sat in the corner, and there was a toilet stall to the side with its own door and a sink near the entrance. I flicked the lock, stripped, and switched on the shower.

Blissful, glorious heat hit my shoulders. I embraced each sting, relieved and, honestly, a little surprised I'd survived the ordeal. Knowing time was of the essence, I scrubbed at my body before finding a bunch of disposable razors in a small cupboard. Before I could step back into the shower to shave around my wound, a gentle knock sounded at the door.

My brows dipped. "I'll be quick." Fuck, I wasn't taking that long.

Another knock and I clenched my jaw, reaching for the lock as I tugged the door open, not giving a shit that I stood starkers. I rocked back on my heels, my frustration disappearing in an instant.

"Matt," I whispered.

His gaze softened a fraction before uncertainty took over. "You mind if I come in?"

Hope bloomed in my chest, only to fade away when he held up a suture kit.

"I thought you might need a hand."

I straightened and pushed aside my disappointment as I took a step back, giving him access. "Sure, thanks."

He locked the door behind himself before turning back to me.

We stood in awkward silence, him assessing my body—likely my injuries—me wondering why I couldn't just open my trap and tell him I was staying. That I wanted to kiss him.

"You, uhm… need help shaving the wound?"

His nerves sent a flutter to my chest.

"That'd be great," I answered despite being able to manage perfectly fine by myself. But hey, if the man was offering to get up close and personal with my naked body, I had no issues with that.

His lips twitched, but he didn't call me out. After all, he'd offered.

"You want to get back in the shower so we can get some suds on your chest?"

When faint pink touched his cheeks, I nodded immediately, voice dropping as I said, "Won't you get wet?"

The pink deepened, flushing to a colour I enjoyed seeing far too much on his usually pale skin.

Wordlessly, he dropped the suture kit on the basin and shrugged off his clothes.

Well, fuck.

I eased back under the spray, unable to look away.

He was glorious.

He stepped into the shower, and as the water cascaded over his body, it washed away some of the grime and blood, revealing the full extent of his injuries. Angry red cuts crisscrossed his chest, some partially healed, others still fresh. Bruises marred his skin, painting a story of the fierce battle we had just survived. Yet, despite the wounds, he was breathtakingly beautiful—lightly muscular, strong, and fuck, he was gorgeous.

My breath caught in my throat as he moved

closer, the space between us shrinking. My body reacted instinctively, heat pooling in my core as I reached for him. He met me halfway, our bodies pressing together under the warm spray. His skin was slick and warm against mine, every point of contact sending electric sparks through my veins.

His eyes, dark with desire, locked onto mine. The weight of what we had faced, the reality of our mortality, hung heavy in the air. We could have died today. This could have been one of our last moments together, and that realisation fuelled the fire between us.

Before I could speak, his hands cupped my face, and his mouth crashed onto mine with a ferocity that took my breath away. The kiss was desperate, filled with pent-up passion and an urgent need to feel alive. I responded in kind, my hands roaming over his body, feeling the hard planes of his muscles, the rough edges of his wounds. My heart pounded in my chest, each beat echoing the unspoken fear of losing him. What could have been.

We kissed harder, more fiercely, the intensity of our emotions driving us to the brink. The steam from the shower enveloped us, creating a protective cocoon. His hands tangled in my hair, tugging me closer as his lips moved hungrily over mine. I could taste the salt of his sweat, the metallic tang of blood, and something uniquely him.

A loud knock on the door shattered our moment, pulling us back to harsh reality. "Wheels up in fifteen minutes, and others need the facilities," a voice called out.

We pulled away reluctantly, breathing heavily, skin flushed. The urgency of our situation pressed down on us, and unspoken questions lingered in the air between us.

"Matt," I whispered, my voice barely audible over the sound of the water.

"Let's get this done quickly. Get you shaved. Then I'll stitch you up out of the room to free it."

He was right, but that didn't mean I had to be happy about it.

"Fine," I grumbled, my cock bobbing between us. It brushed his stomach, and he groaned, eyes dilating.

"Ethan." He bit his bottom lip, peering between us, eyeing my erection. Then he stepped back, shaking his head. "Perhaps this will go faster if you shave yourself and I meet you out there?" He hooked a thumb behind him in the direction of the door.

Feeling cocky, I grinned. "Unable to resist me?"

When he dragged a slow glance down my body,

my gut tightened. He was absolutely the one in control here.

"Maybe. Perhaps we can find out when we get to Sydney."

My brows shot high. Had Tarka told him?

Without another word, he flicked one last longing glance at my cock before he turned, shoved the shower curtain to block his view, got dressed, and hightailed it out of the room.

My laugh remained, loud and satisfied, from the moment he tried to hide me away until deep chuckles followed as I dried and dressed, eager to track him down to discover what exactly he meant by his comment about Sydney.

CHAPTER 11

LUCAS

This was a bad idea.

After I'd been unceremoniously told about Ethan not only being offered a job but accepting it, meaning he was officially relocating, my mind spun out. While ruled by blurring thoughts and possibilities, I'd invited him here. My home.

What on earth had I been thinking?

With his heat at my back, a shiver ran through me, my shoulders sagging a little.

"If you need me to book into a hotel…."

I dropped my head, trying to get myself together before saying, "It's okay. I want you here."

And I did. That didn't mean walking into my private space wasn't going to go seriously wrong. Once invited in, there'd be no going back. No pretending.

Though when Ethan's warm, steady palm pressed against my lower back in silent support, I suspected he already knew I wasn't as put together as I led everyone to believe.

"You can trust me."

The words did the trick, honesty ringing as pure as a bell in the stillness of the night. While my fear didn't subside, it eased a fraction. Ethan had already taken care of me and stepped up when he didn't have to. And not once did I believe he thought any less of me.

Far from it.

He seemed to relish the action, enjoy being there for me.

"Okay," I mumbled, letting him interpret my response however he wished.

I unlocked the first security door, which led to a small lobby. I sensed him looking around and taking in my space as well as the systems I had in place.

A retina scan and a code later, we stepped into the main area—the outer sanctum that I'd previously opened up to my team when I needed to. It was all gleaming surfaces while being comfortable and modern. Off to the side was a large workroom decked out with a wall of screens and multiple workstations my team and I had spent time using before when our base had been compromised.

"Nice digs."

We made eye contact, and a gentle smile formed.

"You want to show me the real you?"

I tugged the inside of my cheeks between my teeth, uncertainty battling with relief. "What do you mean?"

Arching his brow, Ethan tilted his head as he reached out and took my hand in his. "Matt, you can trust me."

There was no denying the small tremble in my hand. No hiding my nerves as they rolled off me, no doubt changing my scent.

With a single nod, I bypassed the door that led to the guest suite. After working through another round of security, the door opened into my private suite: an open-plan area containing a sitting room and dining space, plus a kitchen that featured high-tech mod cons. The bedroom door was closed, which led the way to the large bathroom. I glanced around, trying to imagine my reaction if I saw it for the first time.

A rush of emotions threatened to consume me as we stepped in fully before closing the door at my back, vulnerability mixing with relief. The retina scan and the code had granted Ethan access to a part of me I never revealed.

Not ever.

This space was a stark contrast to the carefully

curated exterior; it was a raw reflection of my internal chaos and solitude.

The living area, though equipped with all the comforts of modern design, was in disarray. There was barely any furniture, and what remained was buried under a mountain of takeout boxes and disposable cutlery. My clothes were strewn across the floor, discarded in moments of exhaustion and indifference. The kitchen, which could have impressed any Michelin-trained chef with its state-of-the-art appliances, was instead coated in a layer of dust and cluttered with empty containers.

My apartment was no longer picture-perfect but a testament to neglect and abandonment.

Yet, despite the mess, it was mine—a space where I could cast off the weight of the world. Here, I could disappear from the expectations and demands that weighed heavily on my shoulders. It was where I would eat, then crawl into bed, or sometimes just collapse on the sofa, surrounded by a nest of blankets and pillows. The sofa felt less lonely than my sterile bedroom, where solitude only intensified my worries and overthinking.

"So this is it." I kept my arms at my side, forcing myself to stand still.

Ethan's presence was both a comfort and a challenge. His expression was carefully controlled as he observed my chaotic environment. Instead of recoiling or passing judgment, he stepped closer, his towering form wrapping me in a solid embrace. He just waited, absorbing what it meant to be part of my life, to understand me.

"I—" How on earth could I explain this?

"I'm exhausted and could happily sleep where I stand." His soft words brushed against the top of my head. "Your sofa looks comfy, and it might handle the two of us."

I sagged against him. "The bedroom's through there."

"You want me to lead the way?"

"Okay." The man I turned into around Ethan, when under his careful scrutiny, I barely recognised. But with such certainty radiating off him, I let him lead the way willingly.

Silently, he picked up the handfuls of clothes off my unmade bed and placed them on my closet floor. Once the bed was clear, he straightened the sheets, a smile slipping onto his lips. "It smells like you."

Heat danced across my skin at the gravel in his voice.

"So I don't need to change the bedsheets?" The tease in my words was instinctive as much as it was a relief.

"Fuck no. Being wrapped around your body as

well as in your scent is going to make it hard as fuck not to maul you and suck an orgasm from you."

A low moan escaped my parted lips.

"But it'll also help me sleep." He dragged his heated gaze down my body. "You want to strip and join me?"

We hadn't discussed anything, not having had a moment to do so. All that had happened since the whirlwind of Victoria was a heavy make-out session in the shower, then, after stitching him up, eating and talking about the case on the flight.

Admittedly that was a lot. Truly so much had happened. But beyond me blurting out the offer for him to come home with me when everyone went their separate ways—including Valeria, who promised to see me tomorrow to talk—I had no clue what was happening.

Thinking about it just added an extra layer of shit I needed to consider, and I didn't know—

"Matt, strip and get your arse into bed."

Instinctively, I narrowed my gaze, preparing to demand he didn't tell me what to do. At his arched brow, the determination in his eyes, and that damn smirk, the urge dissipated, melting as quickly as ice under the outback sun.

We didn't take our eyes off each other as we

stripped. When I got into bed and he pulled the sheet up over me, he made his way to the door.

"Where are you going?" The panic took me by surprise.

I wasn't needy. Ever.

He strolled back to me, his heavy dick swinging in his half-hard state. It was difficult to pull my gaze away when he stopped, groin close to my face. Before I could act on the urge to lean forwards and lick him from top to root, he bent down, his face now close.

"I'm just getting us some water." He searched my gaze. "Do you need blood?"

At the mention of blood, a thirst hit me. It was nowhere near as bad as when we were outside Warwick, but I hadn't drunk enough over the past thirty hours. "There's plasma in the fridge." It was slightly better and more palatable than the synthetic plasma that didn't need to be kept cool, which I relied on when away from the office and home.

He studied me a beat, his gaze carefully assessing. Wordlessly, he dotted a kiss on my lips and left the room, leaving me with my head spinning and pressing my fingers to my lips.

Ethan was likely going to be my undoing. A smirk formed behind my fingers.

I was more than okay with that.

The sound of cupboard doors opening and closing reached me, but rather than tensing up, wondering what he was thinking, the judgments he was making, I relaxed. Ethan didn't strike me as a man who would be anywhere or doing anything unless he wanted to.

Running water followed. When the tap cut off, his footsteps made their way back to my room.

He filled the doorframe, and I frowned, not seeing a plasma vial. He placed a glass of water on the bedside table next to me before heading to the other side. The bed dipped as he lay on the mattress, immediately turning on his side to face me.

My confusion deepened when my gaze roamed his features, seeing uncertainty there. "Are you okay?"

What had happened in the last three minutes to cause nerves to bleed into his expression?

"Yes," he answered immediately.

I waited him out. He had no reason to lie to me.

"Would you… I was…." He huffed out a breath, fresh spearmint from the mints he'd been chewing on the plane like lollies washing over me. "Will you drink from me?"

Shock slammed into me hard, lust quickly following.

Just the thought of tasting him, feeding from him

made it difficult to think of anything but latching onto his neck, his thigh, hell, any part of his body with a throbbing vein.

"You don't have to," he rushed to say, maybe misinterpreting my wide-eyed stare or possibly changing his mind. "Blood from the source is stronger, right? Better?"

His uncertainty melted the hesitation that wound itself around my heart. "Yes. But the plasma vials offer the nutritional value needed."

"I get that." He reached out and tenderly traced my cheekbone and my furrowed brow. "And if I want you to drink from me?"

There was no disguising the shudder of want coursing through my body. His eyes dilated as he eased closer. "Is that something you'd consider?"

I searched his gaze, trying to clear my head. An almost impossibility with the pulse of pheromones rolling off him. "Why?" I all but whispered. "Have you let someone before?" Discomfort sat in my chest with the thought of another vampire sipping at his vein.

Unfair for sure, but true all the same.

"Once. When I was on a training mission and there was a legit life-and-death situation going on."

That he hadn't shared his blood in the heat of passion sent a bolt of lust to my dick.

"Let me take care of you and give you this."

A plea if ever I heard one, the tone doing its job of unravelling me completely. I was eager to give him whatever he wanted.

"Yes." My fangs descended.

His gaze snapped to my mouth, his cock bouncing and trailing slick against my thigh.

My skin tingled, desire unfurling further as I reached out and cupped his cheek. "Kiss me."

His lust-filled gaze softened before he latched his mouth to my waiting lips.

We kissed until he was breathless. We kissed until his heart throbbed in his chest, threatening to break free and join mine.

We kissed until I pushed him onto his back and straddled him, our cocks brushing, weeping, desperate for contact.

Ethan's deep groan reverberated against my skin as his strong hands gripped my hips and rubbed me back and forth against his trapped cock. I could barely think, breathe, remember which way was up as his precum-slicked dick trailed under my balls, against my taint, and between my cheeks, just begging me to reposition and grant him access.

But first….

I pulled away, taking in his kiss-drunk expression. When he bared his neck to me, angling in a way that spoke of complete trust and need, I snapped.

I craved him. Wanted him.

Would do anything for just a taste.

"Do it."

He grunted as I latched onto his neck and sank my teeth into his waiting vein.

A deep, guttural groan tore out of him, his strong arms snaking around my back and holding me close. Tight. It would take a hurricane to tear us apart.

As his blood flowed into me, I embraced the pleasure, the connection, each pulse of his life essence amplifying my senses, making me feel invincible. The warmth of his blood mixed with the undeniable bond between us made the moment intensely intimate.

Every swallow soothed my soul, easing the heartache and the terror of the past few days. Hell, weeks and years. How he pulled such sensations and eased me so was something I refused to question—the possible answer too terrifying and life changing.

Ethan's hands roamed over my body, caressing, exploring, intensifying the heat between us. His every touch ignited my skin, our bodies moving in a rhythm as his hand disappeared. I shuddered at the sound of sucking, anticipation making my blood sing.

His spit-slick fingers split my cheeks, before probing my entrance.

Yes. I angled, opening to him as I allowed myself a final sip.

With each drop, the wounds on my body knitted themselves together, the pain of battle replaced by pleasure. Ethan giving this to me was everything.

A finger breached and I gasped, pulling free from his neck with a feral groan.

"More," I demanded before scooping up the trail of blood seeping from his neck with my tongue.

He pushed in further. In and out. Seeking. Searching. Relentless in his pursuit.

My head swam in ecstasy. His blood seeping into my veins while his second finger breached me, urging me to ride his digits, was too much but nowhere near enough.

I sliced my tongue against my razor-sharp fang before bending down and swiping my blood across the incisions. Satisfied they'd closed, I angled to stare down at Ethan's face.

That he made blissed out look so sexy wasn't a surprise. What had me catching my breath was the softness, the affection in his expression as he peered up at me, his fingers still sliding in and out of me. He didn't speak as he rubbed and moved.

Apparently I didn't have so much control. Not

when he danced his digits over my prostate, sending bolts of pleasure to every cell in my buzzing body.

"Fuck, Ethan," I gasped. "More." I groaned and shuddered. "I need… *nngh*."

"Lube?"

"Drawer," I managed, my half-lidded eyes barely able to focus. "No," I moaned, desperation clinging to my voice at the loss of his fingers.

"Shh… patience."

Manoeuvring my tightly coiled body with ease, he placed me on my back while he rummaged through my bedside table. My cock wept, eager for his attention. One look from him as I trailed my fingers across my stomach, considering wrapping myself in a firm grip, had me pausing.

I came alive under the need, the warning he shot my way. An easy smile quickly formed, the warmth in my chest blooming. I stopped my exploration, receiving a heated smirk followed by one of complete satisfaction as he settled over me, grasping the lube as though he'd returned with some kind of relic.

Wordlessly, he slicked his fingers, his cock. Each sound caused a new eruption of goose bumps as expectation buzzed between us.

Then he was there, finally, digits flirting with my opening, caressing, soothing before he slid fingers deep inside—two or three, I didn't know, didn't care, but the fullness felt right, coiling the urgency for him to drive home.

"Take what you need." The gruff instruction pressed against me, soft and welcoming.

I reacted immediately, tugging his head to mine and kissing him with pent-up need and passion and fear and a desperation that was too much while not being enough. Our tongues stroked and tangled, lips gliding as I bore down, riding his fingers until lightning fired to life in my stomach.

Then I was moving, pulling his fingers away while slamming his strong body onto his back, then clambering on top of him and, for the first time, touching his heavy cock. Thick and warm in my hand, his dick throbbed, the slick melding with the precum dripping out his slit.

Holding him tightly, positioning him exactly where I wanted him, I glanced down, our gazes connecting. Intense eyes peered back at me, full of want and... my gut clenched... delighted amusement? Unable to tell, I hovered, his cock nudging my entrance as I narrowed my gaze.

"Something funny?" I gritted out, swirling my hips so his tip dipped in before easing out. His eye twitched, but I was the one who groaned, edging myself more than him.

"Funny? No." His stare intensified while his cock burned hotter in my hand.

It took every ounce of willpower I had not to slam down and take what we both wanted. Only the unfamiliar pleasure of connection and something real drifting between us stopped me. This teasing was something I'd never experienced before. I wanted to savour every single moment.

"No?" I dipped down again, shuddering as his tip entered, loving the way his neck was corded.

"Definitely not funny." The groan that tore from him as I trailed my fingers down the length of his cock barrelled through me.

Barely having any control left, I sank down an inch, my eyes fluttering closed as I asked, "If not funny, then what?"

"Fuck" burst out of him as he sat bolt upright, holding me steady to give me control so I didn't immediately sink down on him in this new position.

Power radiated from his limbs and his straining muscles. The desire to lick every single one and take my time with him was a genuine quandary. Wanting his cock deep inside me more, I allowed myself a small taste, sucking wet kisses on his shoulder, still smelling the unique tang of his blood.

"You," he moaned, angling his neck to give me better access. "Everything about you, especially you taking what you want...." He grunted when I scraped my fangs across his skin. "It drives me insane. Makes me want to give you everything, even what you don't realise you want or need."

With his words dancing around my mind and wrapping gently about my being, I sagged against him, feeling more of the debilitating weight of thoughts and worries slip away. He held me still, giving me the control to decide when to breach me.

Didn't he already know he consumed me?

I leaned back to stare at him, our heads almost in line in this position.

Our gazes connected, my lips parting when he said, "You make me wish for things I never thought I'd want or deserve."

A loud thump of my heart and I nodded. "Let's chase that together."

It was all the permission he needed. I gave it to him the moment I let go, Ethan reading me with the swift understanding of someone who knew the depths of my soul.

His hands roamed my back with purpose, mapping out every inch as if committing it to memory as I sank down on him. His touch was electric, the fullness of him sending shivers down my spine.

We moved in unison, driven by an unspoken

understanding as I rocked on him and he drove up with firm, deep strokes. Searing kisses consumed me, my skin burning with the imprint of his lips as I rose up, feeling every inch of his cock, living for each sensation as need pulsed through me.

Each pulse of his heart echoed in my veins.

Want.

Need.

Blissful stillness in my head.

Ethan's fingers dug into my flesh, a silent plea for more. I could sense his struggle, the desire to give in to his own pleasure while wanting to be everything I needed. His strength was intoxicating, a heady mix of vulnerability and dominance that made me ache for him even more.

"Ethan," I breathed, my voice barely a whisper against his skin. "I need you."

A storm of feelings darkened his eyes as he looked back at me. "I've got you," he replied, his voice rough with intensity.

His hips moved like a piston as he took hold of my cock. My groan was instant, as were the sparks behind my eyes. Sure, strong strokes followed, picking up speed as my shudders, moans, and pleas increased.

He fucked into me hard, each upswing brushing

against my prostate, every swipe of his hand edging me closer to losing all sense of myself.

Then I was flying. An explosion of sensation. A fusion of our souls. My body trembled with the force of our release—him spilling deep inside and me painting his hand and our chests, branding us both.

"I...." Trailing off, I struggled to process, to speak.

"Shh," he hushed with a gentle kiss against my lips. We wore matching blissed-out grins as he eased us apart as he lay back, tugging me on top of him, our cum warm and sticky between us.

Spent and entwined with him, peace settled over me. My mind still quiet. "Should we...?" I attempted, not making any effort to move.

"No."

I snuggled into his broad, furry chest. "We'll regret it," I mumbled. Dried cum was a pain to scrub clean.

At his "I won't regret anything," I swooned, relieved he couldn't see my goofy smile at the promise filtering his words.

In answer, I dotted a kiss on his chest and let myself fall.

I WOKE FEELING REFRESHED. IT TOOK ME BARELY A second to realise I was alone in bed, and another one for the sound of movement in the kitchen to make me freeze.

Ethan was in my space. In the chaos that offered me comfort. What if he—

I jumped out of bed, barely taking stock of how wonderful my body felt. I threw on a pair of sweatpants, and with my heart in my throat, I stepped out of my room.

Ethan stood in the middle of the disorder of my kitchen, sipping a cup of coffee while the pod machine kicked out another in a disposable cup I didn't recognise. He angled to look at me, a smile forming as he pulled the lip away from his mouth.

"Black and strong, right?"

Mutely, I nodded, trying to figure out what was happening here.

The machine stopped pumping out thick, dark liquid, the silence sounding loud in my cluttered space.

Finding my voice, I asked, "Where are the cups from?"

Turning to me with the second cup in his hand, Ethan handed it over. "The convenience store at the end of the street."

"And my security?"

A smile tilted his lips, a roguish expression forming, telling me all I needed to know.

The arsehole had managed to hack the thing—or at least add himself to the system so he was able to get access.

With a shake of my head, I took the cup and inhaled deeply, my shoulders relaxing even as my gaze roamed the kitchen. "You didn't clean one or go searching?" There was no bite or accusation in my tone, just a need to understand where his head was at.

Two strides and he was in my space, hand at my waist as he peered down at me. "Not my place to mess with your stuff."

I searched his gaze, looking for judgment or dishonesty. Not finding any, my lips twitched. "Thank you."

He bobbed his head before dipping it and stealing a kiss. It was quick but satisfying, as though it was a moment we'd shared a million times.

"I have to head out and start getting shit together."

I wasn't sure of the time, but the sun was barely up. "You're really taking the job?" That he'd just upended his life so quickly was something I struggled to get to grips with. I overanalysed and planned almost every decision I made.

A flash of my blade landing in Maya's chest struck me. Well, almost everything. That move was all instinct. The need to protect Valeria drove me without question or consideration.

I didn't regret the action one bit.

"I am. It felt right when Tarka offered it to me." Intensity shone in his gaze as he studied me, trying, I suspected, to get a read on my reaction.

"Tarka's a good guy."

He nodded slowly, still assessing. "I hope so, since I've signed the contract and uprooted my life."

I chuckled and stepped out of his hold, cupping my coffee with both hands. "Do you do that a lot?" I knew hardly anything about Ethan. Beyond the snippets he shared, I hadn't found much online. When he'd explained why that was—the erasure of his contribution—his reaction, his grudging acceptance as well as the betrayal he felt, had told me a lot about him.

Made me trust him a little more.

"What a lot?"

"Go out on a limb, jump into a decision, consequences be damned?"

He tilted his head. "Are we still talking about the job here or…?"

"I—" Pausing, I offered honestly, "I don't know." My apartment walls pressed down on me, feeling uncomfortable. I wasn't used to people being in my space. Along with all that had happened over the past few days and weeks, it was becoming too much.

Either I needed to disappear into a nest of blankets or get back to work and—

Strong hands on my thighs lifted me high. An undignified squeal that I'd absolutely deny burst out of me. One moment, I was spiralling; the next, my legs were wrapped around Ethan's waist as he took the coffee cup away from me, then drugged me with bone-melting kisses.

I fell willingly into his touch, matching his movements. Every stroke of tongue, each breathless groan, the race to reveal our hard dicks as he backed me against the wall and wrapped his large hand around the both of us.

My head hit the wall with a *thunk*. Hot kisses instantly trailed along my neck as Ethan rubbed against my slit, gathering my precum and adding to his to ease his fast strokes.

"You're going to come," he panted against my neck. "You're going to stop thinking." A long lick followed. "You're going to cover me with your release and know that you can do so every single day."

My balls drew tight, our eyes connecting.

"I'm *sure* about wanting to know you."

Unable to speak, my brain did exactly as directed and whited out.

"I'm *certain* about this move and finding out if we fit as well as I've been dreaming about."

Holy shit.

I grunted, barely hanging on. Wanting exactly what he said.

"Now bite me. Let me know how much you want the same."

I latched on, sinking my fangs into his pulsing vein, drawing deeply. A rush of ecstasy, a flash of rightness as contentment rolled through me along with my release. He shuttled his hand faster, tingles of awareness zapping my skin.

Ethan's rhythm stumbled, and with a grunt, he joined me, coming in hot jets that splashed against us.

I sealed the incisions at his neck, placing a tender kiss there before angling away and looking at him through bleary eyes.

"Better?" He danced his fingers over my stomach, massaging our cum into my skin.

I shuddered, moving my hand and doing the same to Ethan. "Now I am." I smiled, luxuriating in the tease and the goose bumps erupting on his arms.

"Good." He dropped a kiss onto my nose, something no one had done before. My muscles sagged, and I embraced him, absorbing his warmth as he carried me to the bathroom. "Shower, and then I'm pretty sure you have a meeting."

I had several.

I waited for my muscles to lock up, my brain to overload. When I remained a swoony mess in his arms, I sighed, hardly recognising myself.

I was more than okay with that.

* * *

DURRANT WAS THE DICTIONARY DEFINITION OF STOIC. Normally.

For the past thirty minutes, not so much.

"… how many times I can cover for your arses." She shook her head, her frustration seeming to ebb a little.

"To be fair, we never asked for you to cover for us."

I winced before staring at Callen with wide eyes, silently telling him to shut the hell up.

"No, you didn't." Frustration, exhaustion, and a whole jumble of other emotions managed to get wrapped up in her words. "And that right there is the problem. I do it anyway."

Her gaze met mine, and guilt shifted behind my chest. I hated to disappoint people I respected and cared about. There were few people I didn't want to hurt more than Durrant. While my parents lived overseas—I'd never been close to them—Durrant had remained a steadfast support my whole life.

"I am sorry we lied to you," Callen said, sincerity in his voice. "I'm not sorry we lied to get to Melbourne, though."

Durrant's eyes fell closed while I bit the inside of my cheek, wondering at Callen's ability to dig such gigantic holes without a shovel in sight.

"With everything going on," he continued, pointedly ignoring Durrant's long, drawn-in breath, "we couldn't compromise the mission any more."

"Unofficially," she started, taking us in, "if I were in your position, I would have done the same thing, and I hated not being able to authorise it. Too many eyes were on me."

"Officially?" Callen pressed.

"Officially, you should both, along with your team, be put on probation, *but* with the incredible success you had"—I didn't miss the gleam of pride in her eyes. She couldn't say it, but she'd been actively rooting for us—"the SICB and the Australian government are grateful for all you risked and your efforts."

"So that means the ITU will be getting a public apology for the warrants that were out for them?"

Since our unit was meant to be covert, though I'd

begun to lose count of how many people knew of its existence, Callen was totally pushing her.

Durrant appeared to be controlling her reaction, maybe thinking very carefully about her words. "I've already filed my complaints to the necessary people, explaining my disappointment and frustration with the way this case has been handled." Her brow arched as she said, "What I have been able to do is secure additional funding for your division"—she looked at Callen before turning to me—"and the ITU. I made it clear that both are invaluable to the SICB and the country's security. Without continuing to grow and support development in the division, something like this might happen again. The plan is to not let that happen."

My brows shot high.

"We'll talk more about finances later but included will be a discretionary fund for contracting external support in the private sector. Obviously with appropriate security checks and vetting."

I side-eyed Callen. If we'd had the extra resources and support from the likes of Tarka and Eclipse Security, then the whole process of taking down Hornell could have happened so much sooner.

This was huge.

"I've put forth a nominal pay rise for the team,

and next week, we'll meet and discuss the possibility of a new base location."

Durrant glanced at me, and I nodded, more than okay with designing and implementing a new base for the ITU. Excitement shot tingles to my fingers as I considered the tech I could rework to add into the building design and security protocols.

Callen's chuckle and "I think we've lost him" caught my attention.

I looked at him and then Durrant with confusion before I sat a little straighter. Rolling my eyes at Callen, I said a little sheepishly, "I may have a few ideas." Following up with a shrug, I shot them both a "well, what did you expect me to do other than start planning an awesome new lair" look.

"Speak to Daryl when you leave, and we'll organise a time. Start thinking of locations," Durrant instructed, signalling the meeting's end.

As we stood, I said, "No worries," while Callen added, "You don't really need me for that, right?"

I pressed my lips together. Admin meetings were Callen's idea of hell. Honestly, I was sure we were all surprised that he managed to be so good at his role despite being stuck mainly at the division's headquarters.

"Just get the hell out of here." Durrant shooed us

away. "If I don't see your face for a while, Callen, I'm more than okay with that."

Callen grinned. "Sounds good to me, boss." He tugged open the door and left, leaving me to follow.

Durrant's "Agent Lucas" stopped me.

When she indicated the door, I pushed it closed.

Immediately, concern bled into her gaze. Rather than stiffen, I heaved out a breath and smiled tightly. "I'm okay."

Knowing each other as well as we did, words weren't always necessary.

"Valeria and I are meeting later."

"That's good." Durrant shot me a kind smile. "I think she'll be ready to listen." At my confused expression, she clarified, "She stayed with me last night. We talked, but only about things that I was sure she already knew."

That was good. That Valeria had Durrant, someone she'd called aunt since the moment she could speak, was important.

"Thank you."

"And Wilder?"

Just the mention of his name drew an easy smile, my heart constricting with contentment.

"I'm happy for you."

I chuckled. "Thanks. I'm happy for me too. It's

early...." I petered off, not sure I needed to clarify any more.

"I have no doubt everything will work out as it should."

"I hope so," I admitted.

"Perhaps soon you can stop by, have dinner? You're welcome to bring Wilder."

At my surprised expression, she laughed.

I narrowed my gaze. "Does that mean you've already done a background check and reached out to your connections in the UK?"

I didn't buy her carefree shrug at all. There was no way she'd be letting Ethan into her home, let alone say she was happy for me, if she hadn't.

I settled on "Maybe. Let him acclimatise first." I didn't want to scare Ethan off by my surrogate aunt putting the fear of God into him. Though something told me Ethan could handle himself just fine.

"Okay." She smirked. "Take a few days to unwind."

The very mention of the mandatory days off soured my stomach.

"I mean it, Lucas. That and your attendance with the counsellor are non-negotiable."

The latter I had no issue with. I'd killed my ex-wife, the mother of my child, the woman who'd spent years gaslighting me and making me feel insignificant and incapable.

Sure, having Valeria know the truth helped me breathe easier. And having Ethan hold me close and tease and flirt and help me to forget my own name was incredible. But I wasn't foolish enough to think yesterday's events hadn't left a mark.

"I will," I promised.

She waved me off, and I left after securing a meeting time next week to discuss the relocation of the ITU. I grasped onto the pulse of excitement as I headed to Ethan's new home. A lot was happening, so I needed to remember to keep breathing, and checking out Ethan's digs would be a good starting point before I met with my daughter.

CHAPTER 12
WILDER

I TUGGED OUT ANOTHER BEER FROM THE ICEBOX—ESKY, whatever—opened it, and took a deep swig. Having access to the rooftop garden—something only Base and I had use of—was pretty darn awesome. Though what that did mean was, I had no real reason to not throw a "housewarming" party.

Which I'd absolutely tried to get out of. But between my new teammate—an overexcited tiger who had the energy of a ferret on acid that I was reluctantly enjoying getting to know—and Matt, who thought it would be "good for me," I'd folded.

"Since you're offering." Hart sidled up to where I manned the grill, palm outstretched.

I sighed and scooped up a beer to pass him.

"Cheers." He threw me a wink before gulping the

cold beer down. "You need a hand?" He eyed the barbecue.

"Just because you bloody Aussies like to think you're the kings of the 'barbie,' it doesn't mean I don't know how to handle a sausage."

"That's what he said," Michaels hollered from a few metres away.

I flipped him the middle finger. He was lounging on the outdoor seating, Shaw practically attached to his side, and chatting to Base. It was no surprise they got along. They were as unhinged as each other.

Hart snickered at my side, the relaxed, happy sound tugging a smile from me.

"You're an arsehole," I muttered. That would never change, but him being happy and actually finding someone to put up with his sullen arse was a hell of a thing. I flipped the steak, cast a glance at Matt to make sure he was okay, then asked Hart, "You thought any more about Tarka's offer?"

I'd officially completed my first month at Eclipse Security. It hadn't happened without teething problems. When I'd warned my new boss that I didn't play well with others, I hadn't been exaggerating.

I'd pissed people off, rubbed them the wrong way, and become frustrated as fuck with all the rule following, but despite all of that, the whole Sydney team was here celebrating with me. Officially it was because my shipment had finally come in from the UK, which meant I had no more excuses to not invite them over.

Unofficially?

A whole month and I hadn't been fired and I hadn't killed anyone—or anyone me—and I supposed that was something positive to celebrate.

"I'm not sure. Durrant's still got an offer on the table."

Since he didn't look troubled about either the offer or the decision he needed to make, I suspected he'd work things out when he was ready. For the time being, he seemed happy to continue his solo work.

He took another drink of beer before eyeing the grill. "The steaks are burning."

"For fuck's sake," I said, gritting my teeth. I grabbed the plate and piled it high with red meat. "Everyone's a fucking food critic."

He scoffed as I passed him, taking the steaks to the table.

"Looks—" Matt paused, lips curling up. "—well done?"

"Seriously? I'll eat all the damn things myself if you're gonna complain too." I took his plate off him and plonked a large steak down on it with a pointed "if you talk shit about my steak, I'm gonna launch it off this damn roof" look.

He tugged his lips between his teeth. All that did was draw my attention to his mouth rather than get pissy that he was laughing at me. I scooped up some pasta salad and corn on the cob before passing him the heaped plate. "Sit your arse down and eat."

He arched his brow as he took his food. "No garlic bread?"

"Not if you want my cock down your throat later."

A chorus of "Eww…" and "Fuck, man" and "Jesus, TMI" surrounded us.

I grinned, happy with myself, shouting, "Anytime you all want to leave, there are 360 exits all around us," while pink flooded Matt's cheeks.

"You're such an arsehole." He glared daggers at me, but Matt could play coy all he wanted. Not only did he love me looking after him, doing little things like cooking for him and making sure he ate, but the bitching, the grousing… it went hand in hand with the flirting we'd perfected over the past month.

"You know it." I punctuated my words with a smacking kiss, lapping up my new reality. That I had this. Had someone I cared for so completely that embarrassing him with PDAs made me ridiculously happy.

Leaving him with burning cheeks, I headed back to the grill and an amused Hart.

"You know—"

I cut Hart off. "Whatever you're going to say, do I really need to hear it?"

"I forgot how much of a cock you can be."

"You've been missing me, huh? While I've been at my new job, you've had no one to try to beat you at Wordle. I get it."

Hart huffed out a laugh, and I joined in. "You see, right there. It's been hard not listening to you being a huge dick down the line."

Over the years, while our friendship had been tentative and we didn't really collaborate on much, we had fallen into a pattern of throwing shit at each other, and some of that was absolutely over Wordle.

"Even more reason for you to think about branching out." I lifted my hands before me. "And that's all I'll say about you deciding on jobs."

His "I'll think about it" surprised me. Though, truthfully, like me, I didn't expect Hart would ever be truly comfortable working for a government agency again. We'd both been burned, and some scars never faded.

Hiding my smirk, I turned back to the grill and threw on a bunch of burgers. These arseholes were greedy fuckers and packed away so many kilos of meat, I was going to look into buying shares in livestock.

When Valeria approached, Hart excused himself.

"Was it something I said?" Amusement coloured her tone.

"I think that was all me." I threw her a smile. "You want a drink?" I eyed the orange juice in her hand.

"I wish. I'm doing the whole supportive thing with Tess."

Nonplussed, I shook my head. I'd met her fiancée, Tess, several times now. With Valeria's assignment over—simply good timing that she was able to answer Durrant's call a month ago—Tess and Valeria had moved back to Sydney.

I was happy for Matt. His relationship with his daughter, while strained, was getting easier every day. They'd talked and cried, even attended a couple of therapy sessions together. They still had a way to go, but considering only a month had passed since they'd reconnected, I was confident they'd make it work.

That Tess was all for the reunion helped a hell of a lot.

"You know, not drinking alcohol while she isn't?" She arched her brow.

I scrunched my brow. "Does she have a—" Fuck,

what was the PC term to use, or at least the phrase I could use without insulting someone? This right here was why I was shit at peopling. "—uhm… an unhealthy relationship with booze?"

A burst of surprised laughter erupted as Valeria shook her head. "Well, if you can call her being pissed off that she can't neck a bottle of wine after she's finished her shift at the hospital unhealthy, then yeah, sure."

"O-kay?" I glance around, searching for anyone who could help me. Matt's gaze focussed on me before turning to his daughter as he stood, his eyes wide.

The hell was wrong with him? Why did he look like he'd seen a—

"Ohh…." Understanding dawned a moment before I did a double-take, seeking out Tess first, who sat on the couch, also peering over at us, amusement on her face. "Holy shit, you guys are pregnant?"

All conversation cut off, and I winced. Though, to be fair, every single person currently out here had supernatural hearing. Even if I'd whispered, anyone tuned in would have heard.

My brows shot high, and once again I sought out Matt. He'd been making his way over when I'd blurted the words out.

At Valeria's "Yes, we're pregnant" and her huge-arse grin, I smiled at Matt.

"I'm going to be an uncle again?" Michaels broke in before anyone else could speak. "Fuck yes. Nice." He glanced around, thoroughly pleased with himself.

Meanwhile, I hugged Valeria, feeling kind of awkward. But this was what I thought people did. "Congratulations."

She patted me back just as awkwardly, making me feel marginally better, as her dad and Tess reached us. Matt was already hugging his future daughter-in-law, his eyes glistening as he stared over Tess's shoulder at Valeria.

"This is incredible." He broke free from Tess, offering her a blinding smile before unceremoniously wrapping his daughter in a giant hug. "I'm so happy for you both."

My heart constricted at the love in his voice, his gaze, the way he poured such easy affection into holding his daughter.

He was incredible and so fucking beautiful, especially like this with emotion in his eyes. Easing away after kissing Valeria's cheek, he released her, watching as the two women joined hands, their excitement contagious.

"Looks like you're going to be a grandfather in

approximately six months," Valeria said with a teasing lilt.

Matt shook his head, not in denial but in clear disbelief. "I—" His voice broke.

I was there in an instant, at his side, arm around him, my hand at his waist. Matt was incredible and had been working hard to find balance. It helped him stop getting overwhelmed.

Sometimes, though, and I suspected for a long time to come, I held him up, reminded him he wasn't alone and that he could lean on me. Just like he supported me, especially with the difficulties of fitting in and finding my place at work.

But loving Matt was easy.

My shoulders stiffened, the reality slamming me in the face.

I loved him.

Concern filled his eyes when he glanced my way.

I relaxed my shoulders and fixed a cocky smile. "Granddad, huh?"

It was clear he didn't buy my shift from the hard look he captured me with. Not calling me out, he shook his head. "That doesn't mean I'm old. Just lucky."

So was I.

I pressed a kiss on the top of his head in silent agreement.

Valeria saying, "We'll see if you're both saying that when you're on grandchild-sitting duty. We'll see how quickly they can wrap their granddads around their finger," pulled me up short.

My lips parted, heart pummelling my chest.

Shit. Was I freaking out? I shouldn't be freaking out, but hell, me, a grandfather?

"I can barely pick up a glass bowl without breaking it" tumbled out of my mouth.

I was sure I heard Hart snort, but I couldn't even begin to think about seeking him out to flip him off.

Tess pressed her lips together while Valeria shook her head. "You won't break our kid. You'll be fine."

But how could she be sure?

"And on that note, I'm going to leave you to talk this out." Valeria walked away to talk to the rest of the team, receiving hugs and congratulations while Matt guided me off the rooftop and into my apartment, only stopping once we were in my bedroom with the door closed.

"Butt on the bed, Ethan."

I did so without question, my heart still pounding too loudly.

"You want to talk about—"

"I can't be trusted with a kid," I said quickly, horror in my voice.

Matt's brows jumped high. Ignoring my outburst

for a moment, he pushed my legs open and stood between them. With one hand on the back of my neck in a soft hold, he glided the fingers of his other hand through my hair. We stayed like this for a while, the gentle strokes soothing, encouraging me to calm my racing heart.

Once it finally beat at the normal rate and my head no longer buzzed with panic, Matt cupped my cheek and arched his neck so he could meet my gaze.

"You don't have to be my grandbaby's grandfather. You don't have to be involved at all." Not a single hint of disappointment or accusation existed in his tone. "Whatever you're worried about, if you can tell me, I'd be happy to listen."

This man was perfect. He was complicated and messy and so kind and giving. And so fucking smart and sexy. I wanted everything with him.

"Give me a sec," I managed, trying to get my thoughts straightened out and figure out why I'd balked so damn dramatically. I'd be embarrassed if I gave a shit about what anyone but Matt thought.

"Okay." He continued to card his fingers through my hair, gently massaging my scalp as he did so. I sighed into the touch, absorbing the contact and using it to help centre me.

He gave me time, which I'd known he would. It was that ease—the understanding, acceptance, and respect we showed each other—that helped me draw in a breath.

"You know why I chose a solitary life." I glanced up and he nodded. It wasn't like it was a big secret. I'd loved and lost and been left behind. It wasn't even like it was at an early age. But somewhere along the way of growing and living, being let down by the cyber team in the worst possible way, it became easier to not give a shit.

Matt knew all this. His eyes sparkled with empathy as he remained silent, gently trailing his fingers over the back of my neck.

"You're giving me so much to lose." I dropped my gaze, frustrated with the emotion in my voice.

Not forcing me to speak, Matt waited me out until I was able to look up and meet his eyes.

"I love you."

At my confession, his lips parted, his breath hitching, his chest expanding.

"If I was kicked out of the team, I'd be pissed. If you told me you wanted to split, I'd be crushed. But add in a baby, me becoming a granddad, and have it taken away… a family…." I trailed off and shook my head, a tear spilling free and landing in my beard. "I'm not sure I could survive a loss like that."

I wasn't sure what I expected, but a blinding grin wasn't it.

Matt cupped my face with both hands, his eyes glistening with unshed tears. "I love you so fucking much."

A burst of surprised laughter escaped me. Fuck, I loved it when he swore.

"That you're shit scared of loving my daughter, our grandkid, our family—that's one of the reasons I love you so damn much."

"I didn't say I was shit scared," I grumbled, grasping the words like a lifeline to dry up my tears.

"Uh-huh." When he kissed me, I tasted salt. "But you did say you loved me."

My shoulders sagged even as my chest expanded with the love bottled inside it. "I did. I do."

"And you want to be a family."

A statement that had me slowly nodding. But…. "Just to be clear, that means Vally and Tess and the kid, right? Not us looking at adding our own extra kids?"

He laughed loud and hard, almost bending double. No doubt at the horror I couldn't keep from my face or my voice.

"You finished?" I asked gruffly, only smirking a little when I took control and manoeuvred him to straddle me.

Wrapped around me, he wiped the tears from his

face like the arsehole he was. "Just us, and any other kids *they* may want. Plus, you know who…."

I sighed and pressed my head to his chest with a groan. "Do you really expect me to start thinking about your pain-in-the-arse team as family? It seems unnecessarily cruel."

He chuckled and kissed the back of my head. "Yes, and at some point, maybe you'll start feeling the same about Eclipse?"

My snort was loud. "It's like you hardly know me at all." I looked up, appreciating how right he felt in my arms.

"I think I know you well enough to tell Valeria to organise the 'Best Granddad' tees that I'm confident she already has planned."

Knowing Valeria, she absolutely would, just to screw with us.

"And I absolutely know you well enough that you might scoff at the idea of wearing a T-shirt like that, but you'd do so in a heartbeat, especially if it'll make me smile."

I shook my head slowly before leaning up and tugging his lip between my teeth, earning me a hiss before I let go, saying, "You really are the worst ever."

"Or the best." His smile was wide. "Depends how you look at it."

That sounded like a challenge.

With a lift and a flip, I got him flat on his back on my bed. He landed with a grunt and a chuckle.

"How about I look at it from up here as I take you apart and help you forget your name?"

At Matt's breath hitch, a fresh wave of warmth pressed down on me.

"You have guests upstairs."

"*We* have guests upstairs, since you invited them," I said, not giving a damn about anyone other than Matt and seeing him naked.

"Still, they're upstairs."

A slow, salacious smile fluttered across my lips. "Let's see how long it takes for them to fuck off when they start hearing you scream my name."

Skin flushed, Matt stared up at me, not doing a single thing to argue.

Bliss, just out of reach, kept him still. But he knew I'd take care of him. I always would.

And right now, I'd do that by making good on my promise to tug as many screams from him as possible. His orgasm was mine, and as I kissed his stomach, making my way to his waistband, I breathed him in, barely believing how my life had changed.

A new country, job, friends, a family, and a love that would grow stronger every day… I unbuckled Matt's belt, relishing the burst of pheromones.

This man right here, he was it for me. And I'd do anything to make sure we got through this complicated thing called life together.

BE SURE TO CHECK OUT MY SOCIALS AND STAY UP-TO-date with my upcoming releases as you'll definitely see the ITU team again—most likely in a spin-off series.

If you're new to this series, be sure to check out Callen and Thatch's story, . If you're looking for more Aussie romances, my Outback Boys series is a fun series to read.

ACKNOWLEDGMENTS

I have absolutely adored writing every single words of the Fangs & Felons series. Thank you for sticking with me. And a gigantic thank-you especially to Lana and Cat, who encouraged me to see this series through.

A big shout out to my wonderful team who support me from concept to publication—CC, Barb, Claire at BookSmith Design, Gel at Tempting Illustrations, and my team of Hot Tree Editing editors and support staff. I couldn't do any of this without such wonderful support.

A special thanks to my folks, who rallied around me when I was on a time crunch and hand-delivered meals and glasses of wine to me when I was writing.

ABOUT THE AUTHOR

I live and breathe all things book related. Usually with at least three books being read and two WiPs being written at the same time, life is merrily hectic. I tend to do nothing by halves, so I happily seek the craziness and busyness life offers.

Living on my small property in Queensland with my human family as well as my animal family of cows, sheep, chooks, and dogs, I really do appreciate the beauty of the world around me and am a believer that love truly is love.

To check for updates head to my website:

HTTPS://BECCASEYMOUR.COM

HTTPS://LANDING.MAILERLITE.COM/WEBFORMS/LANDING/R9F0I4

Plus, join my Facebook group, which I share with the awesome Louisa Masters here:

HTTPS://WWW.FACEBOOK.COM/GROUPS/ROMMANCEWITHBECCALOUISA/

Join me on Patreon: patreon.com/BeccaSeymour

facebook.com/beccaseymourauthor

x.com/beccaseymour_

instagram.com/authorbeccaseymour

bookbub.com/authors/becca-seymour

tiktok.com/@beccaseymourwrites